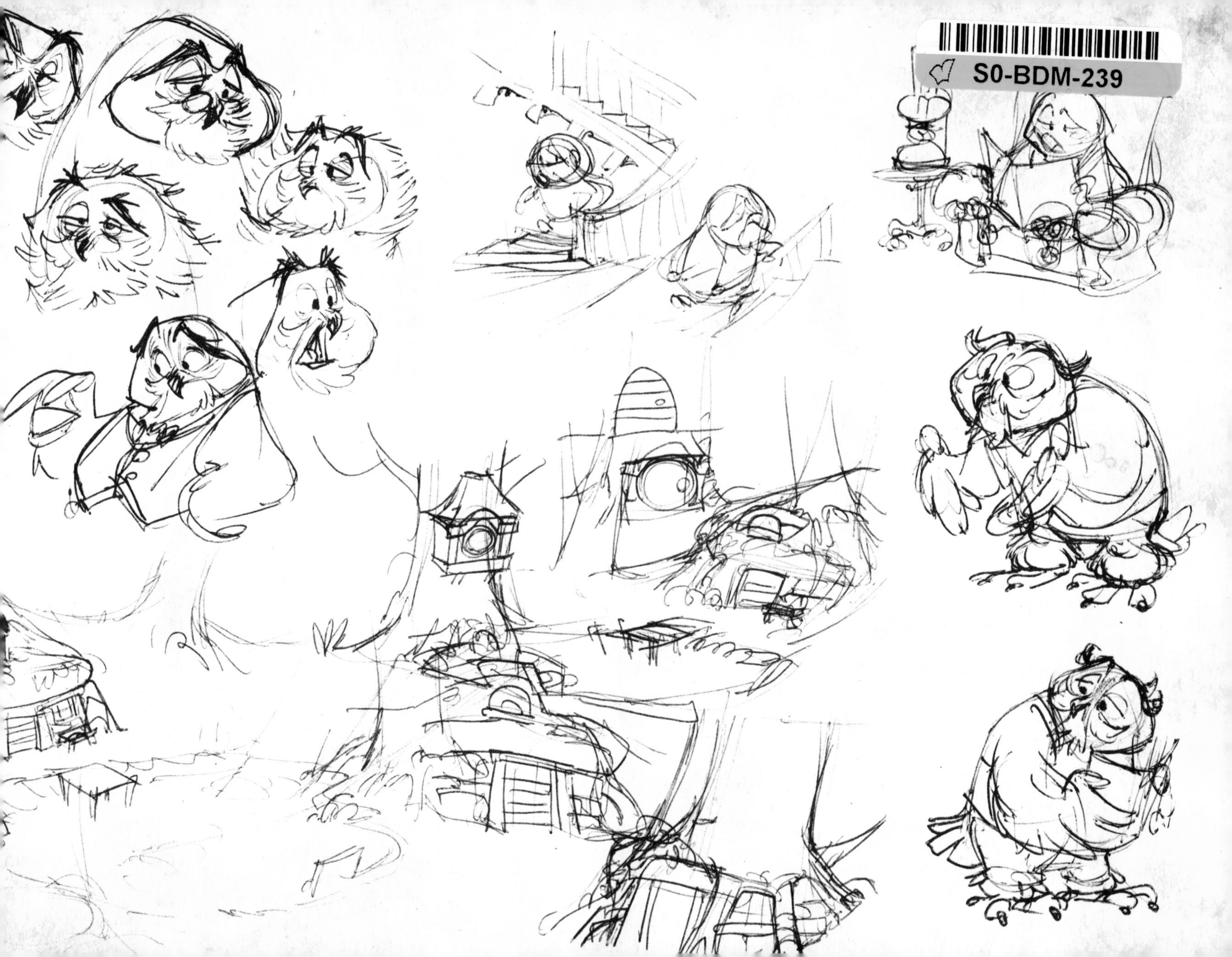

Beneath the Trees

DAV

Trees

A FINE SUMMER

MAGNETIC PRESS

Written and illustrated
by
DAV

*Thank you to the Gouttière team for their passion
as well as to all the Disney artists for the inspiration...*

And thank you for choosing this book!
— **Dav**

Translation, Layout, and Editing by Mike Kennedy
Production Assistance Chris Northrop

ISBN: 9781951719548
Library of Congress Control Number: 2021923549

Beneath the Trees: A Fine Summer, Published 2022 by Magnetic Press, LLC.
Originally published as *SOUS LES ARBRES 3 - Un chouette été* © Éditions de la Gouttière 2021, by DAV.
www.editionsdelagouttiere.com All rights reserved.
MAGNETIC PRESS™, MAGNETIC™, and their associated distinctive designs are trademarks of Magnetic Press, LLC. No similarity
between any of the names, characters, persons, and/or institutions in this book with those of any living or dead person or institution is
intended and any such similarity which may exist is purely coincidental.

Printed in China.
10 9 8 7 6 5 4 3 2 1

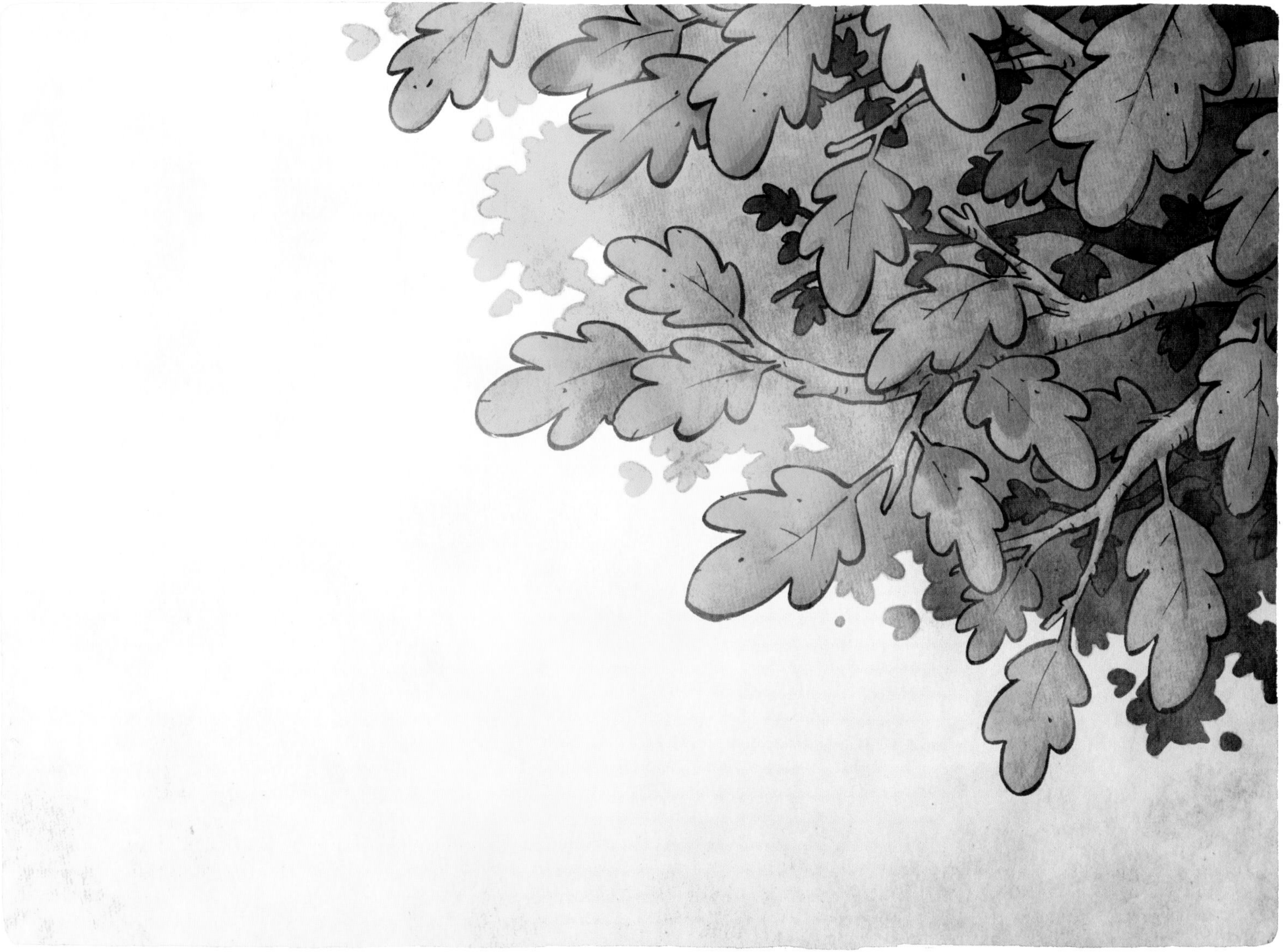

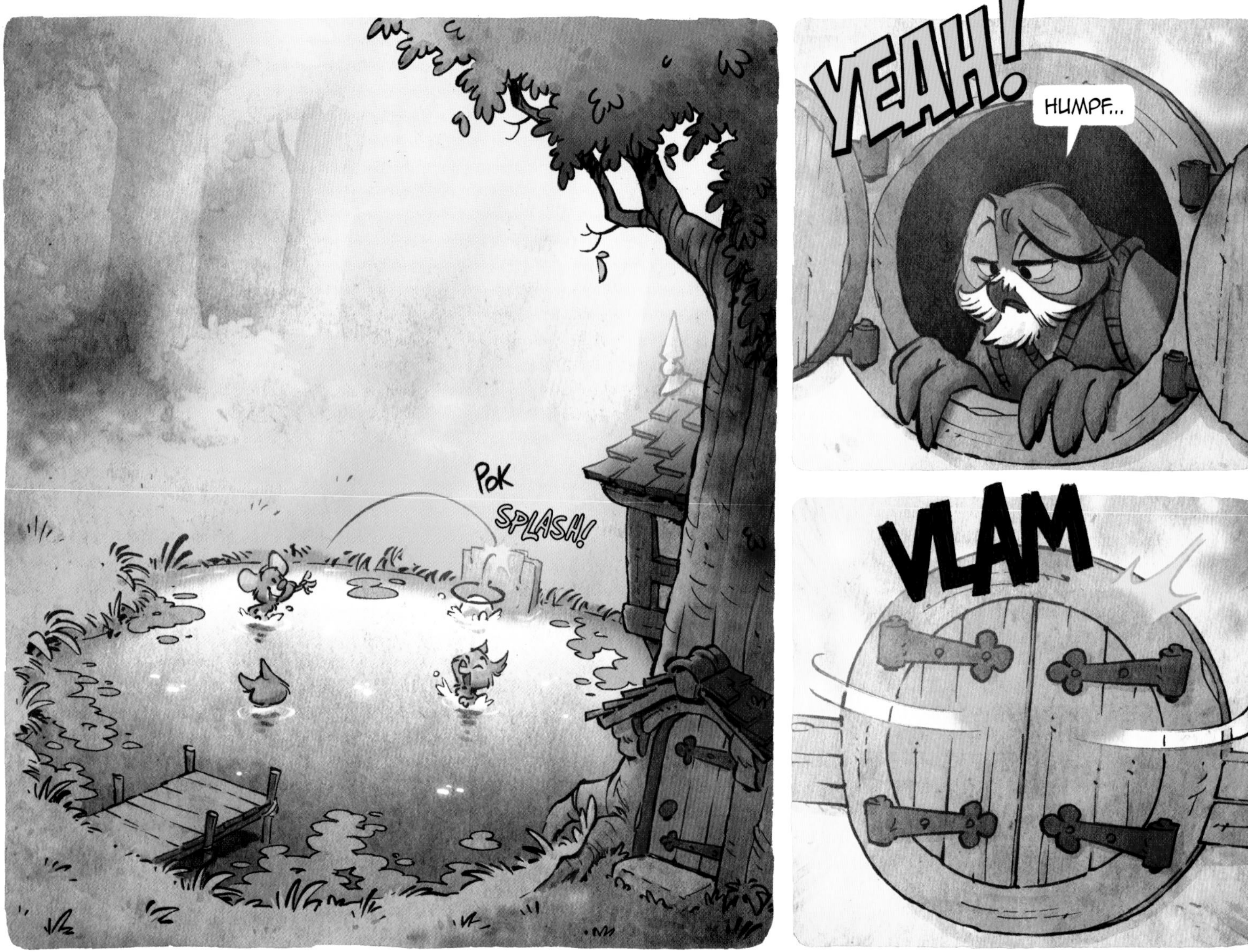
POK
SPLASH!
YEAH!
HUMPF...
VLAM

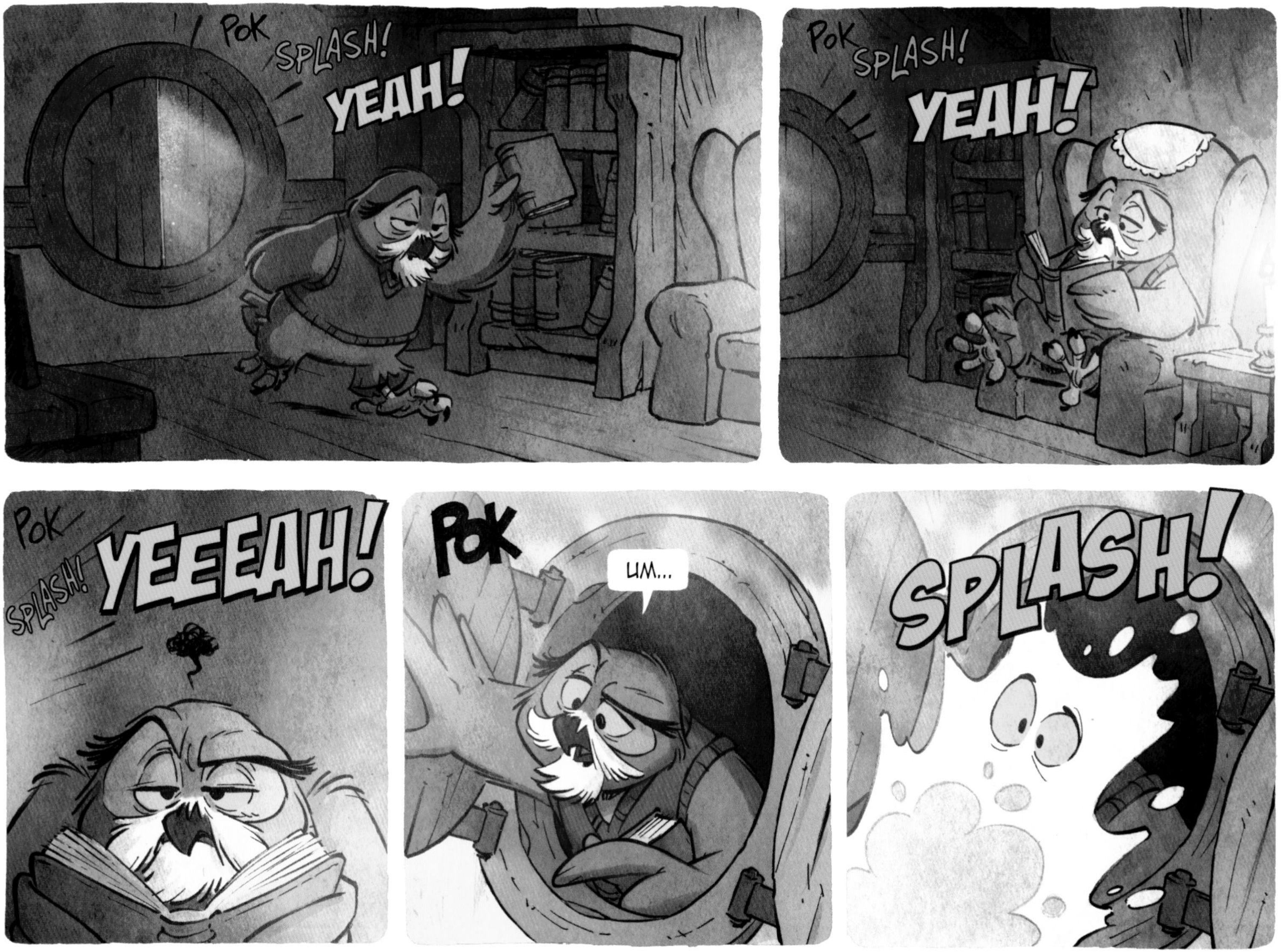
POK
SPLASH!
YEAH!
POK
SPLASH!
YEAH!
POK
SPLASH!
YEEEAH!
POK
UM...
SPLASH!

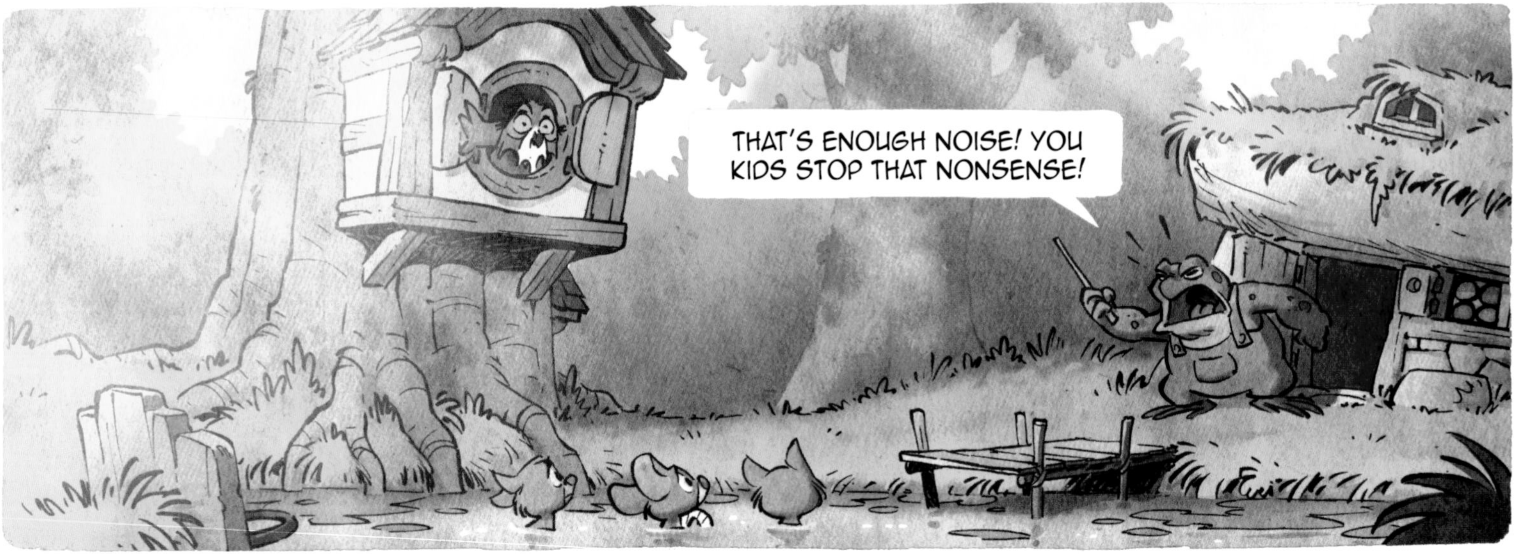
THAT'S ENOUGH NOISE! YOU KIDS STOP THAT NONSENSE!

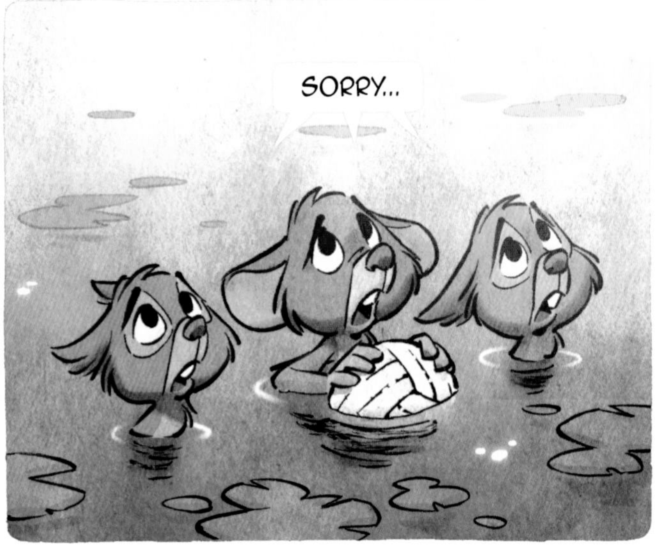
SORRY...

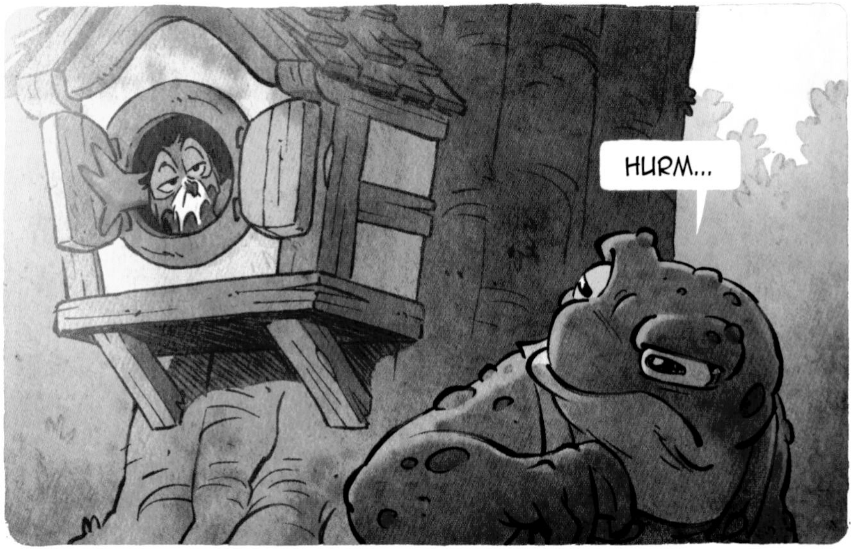
HURM...

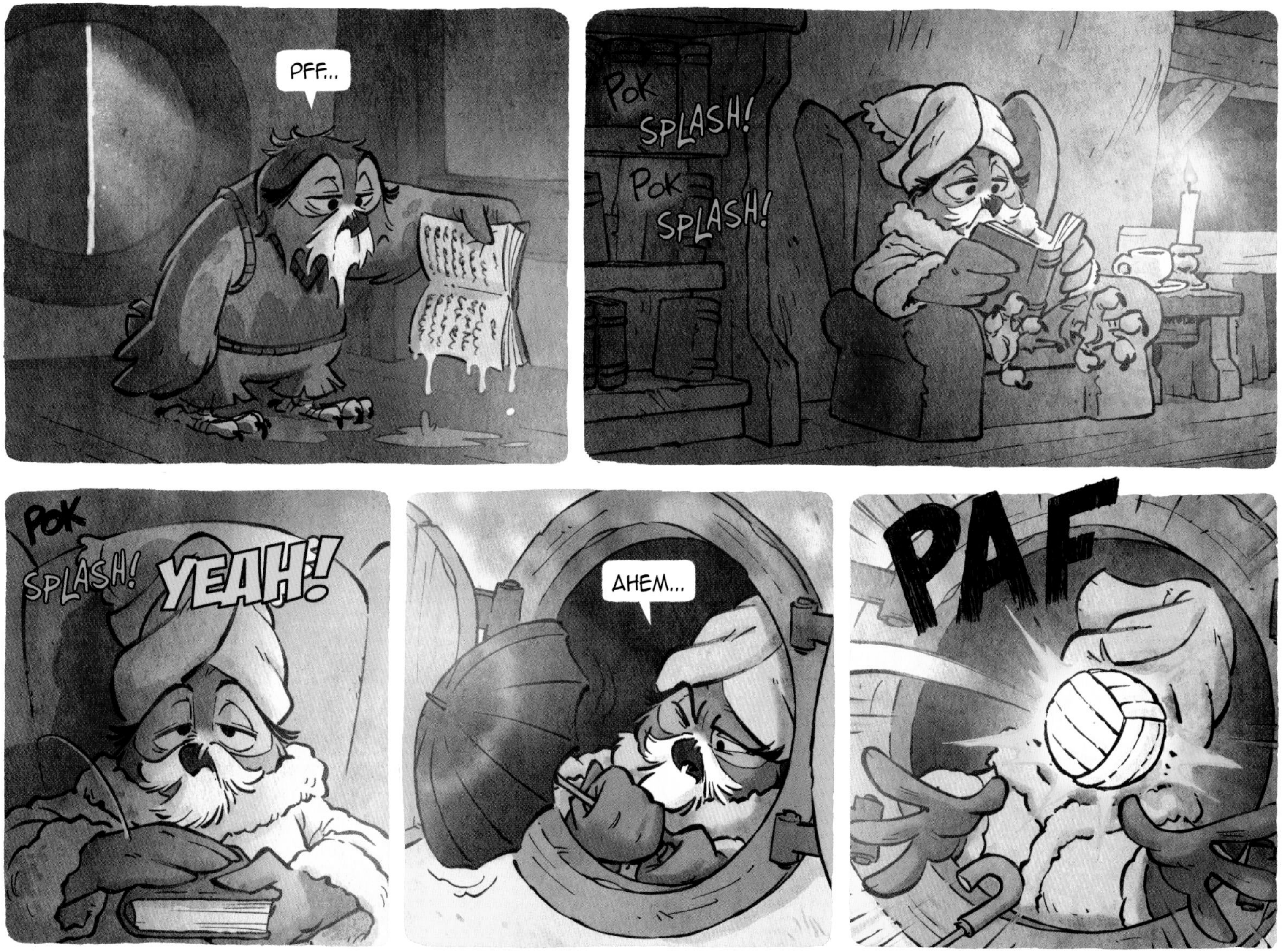
PFF...
POK
SPLASH!
POK
SPLASH!
POK
SPLASH!
YEAH!
AHEM...
PAF

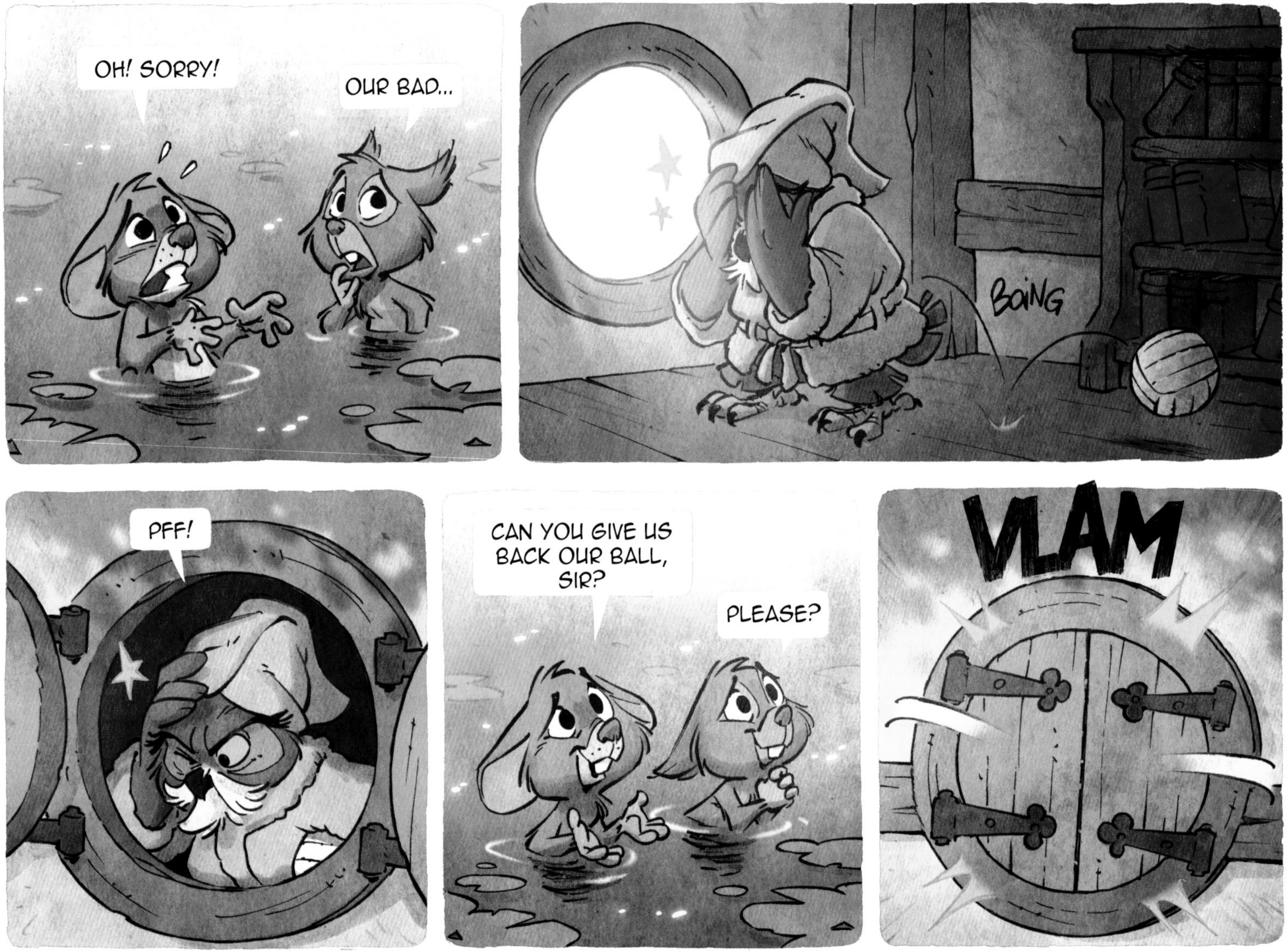
OH! SORRY!
OUR BAD...
BOING
PFF!
CAN YOU GIVE US BACK OUR BALL, SIR?
PLEASE?
VLAM

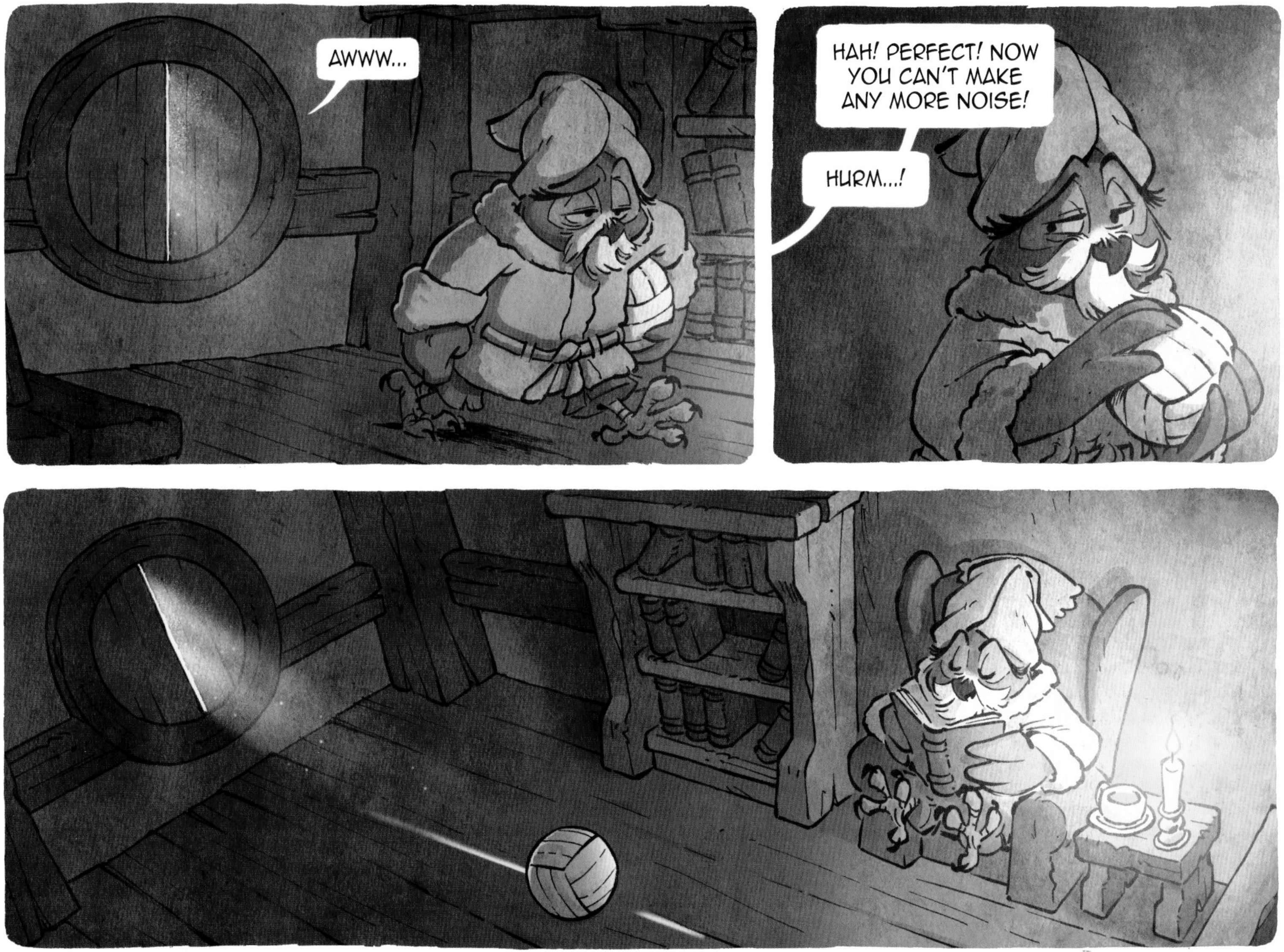
AWWW...
HAH! PERFECT! NOW YOU CAN'T MAKE ANY MORE NOISE!
HURM...!

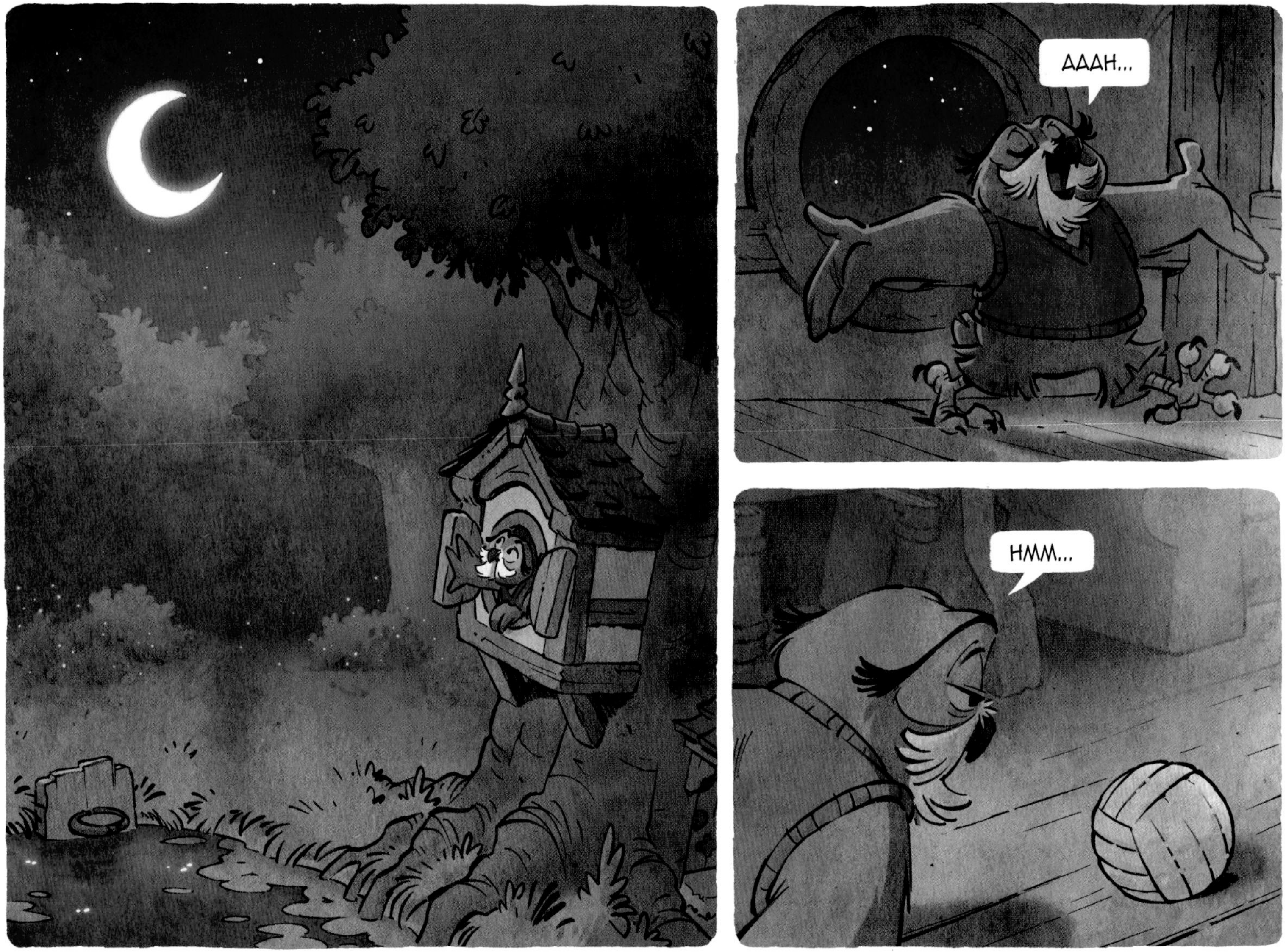
AAAH...
HMM...

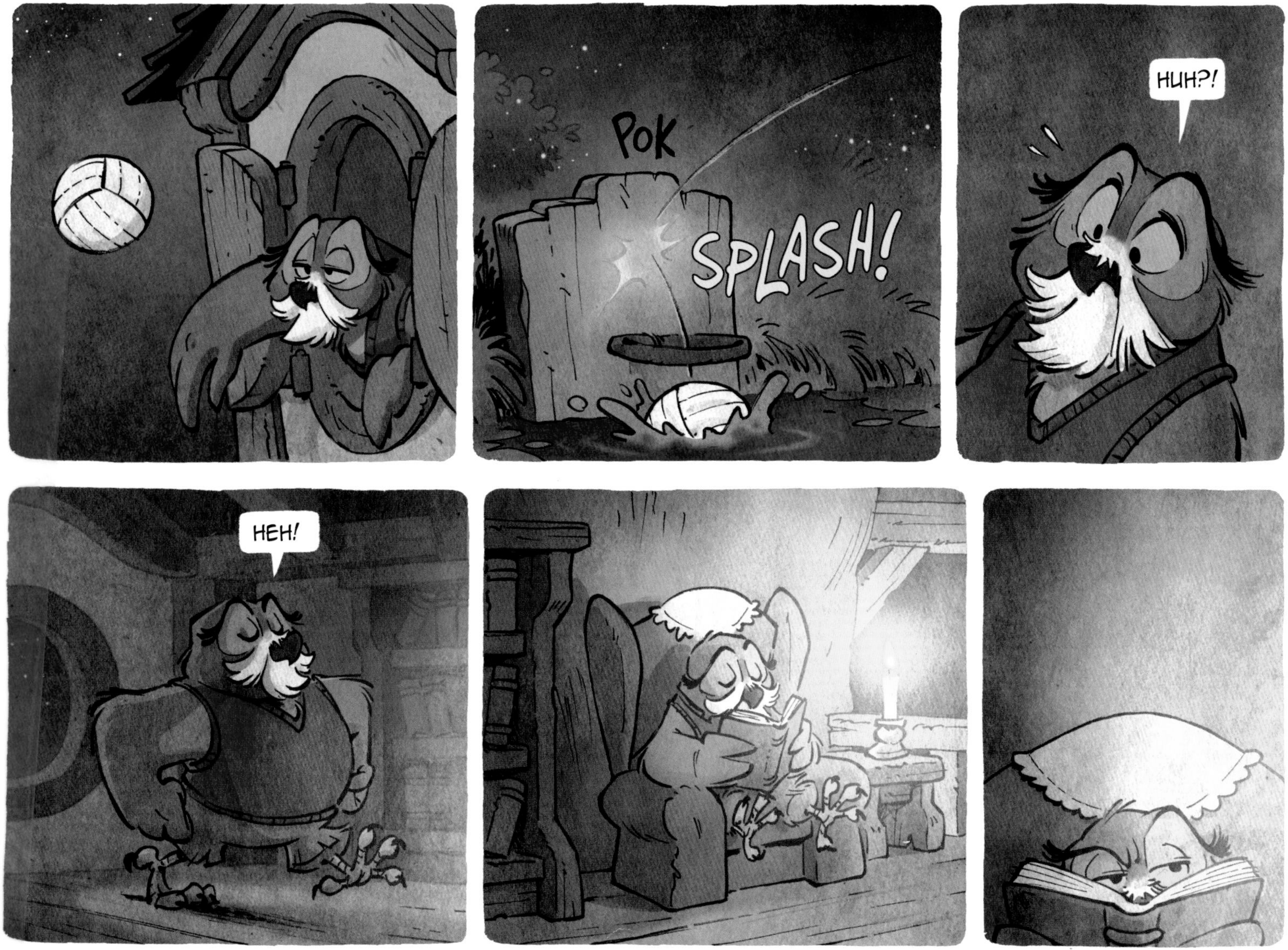
POK
SPLASH!
HUH?!
HEH!

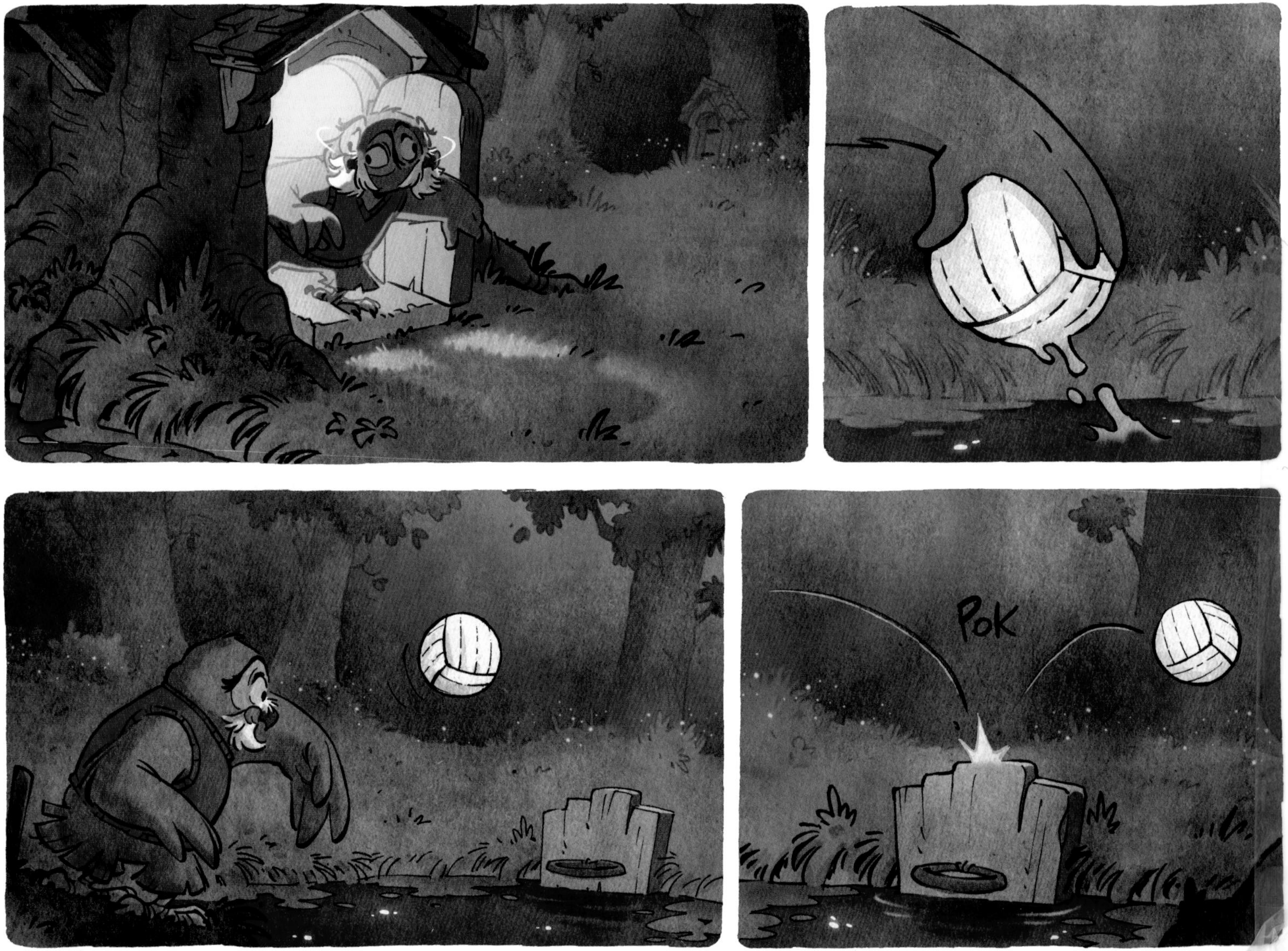
POK

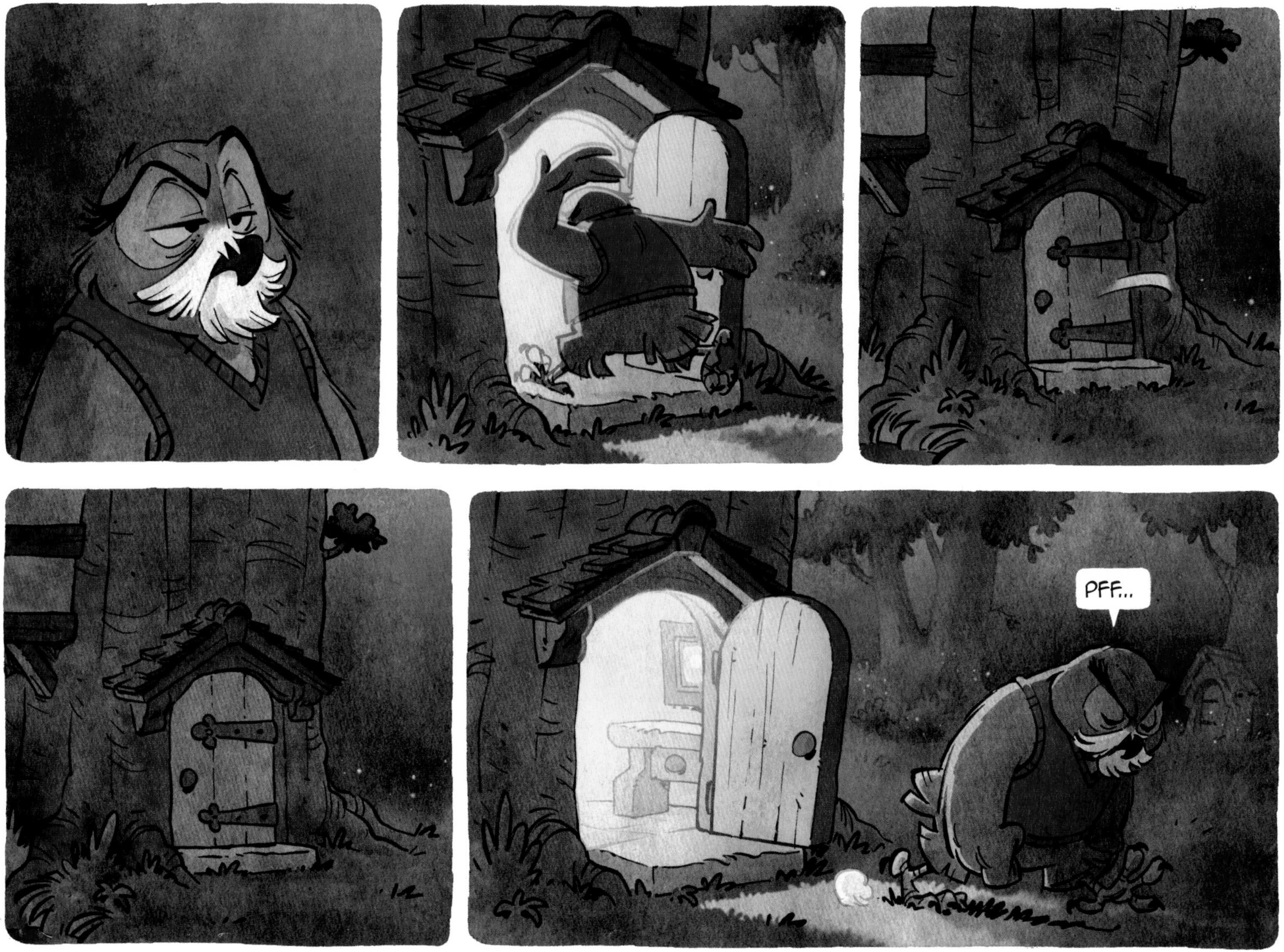
PFF...

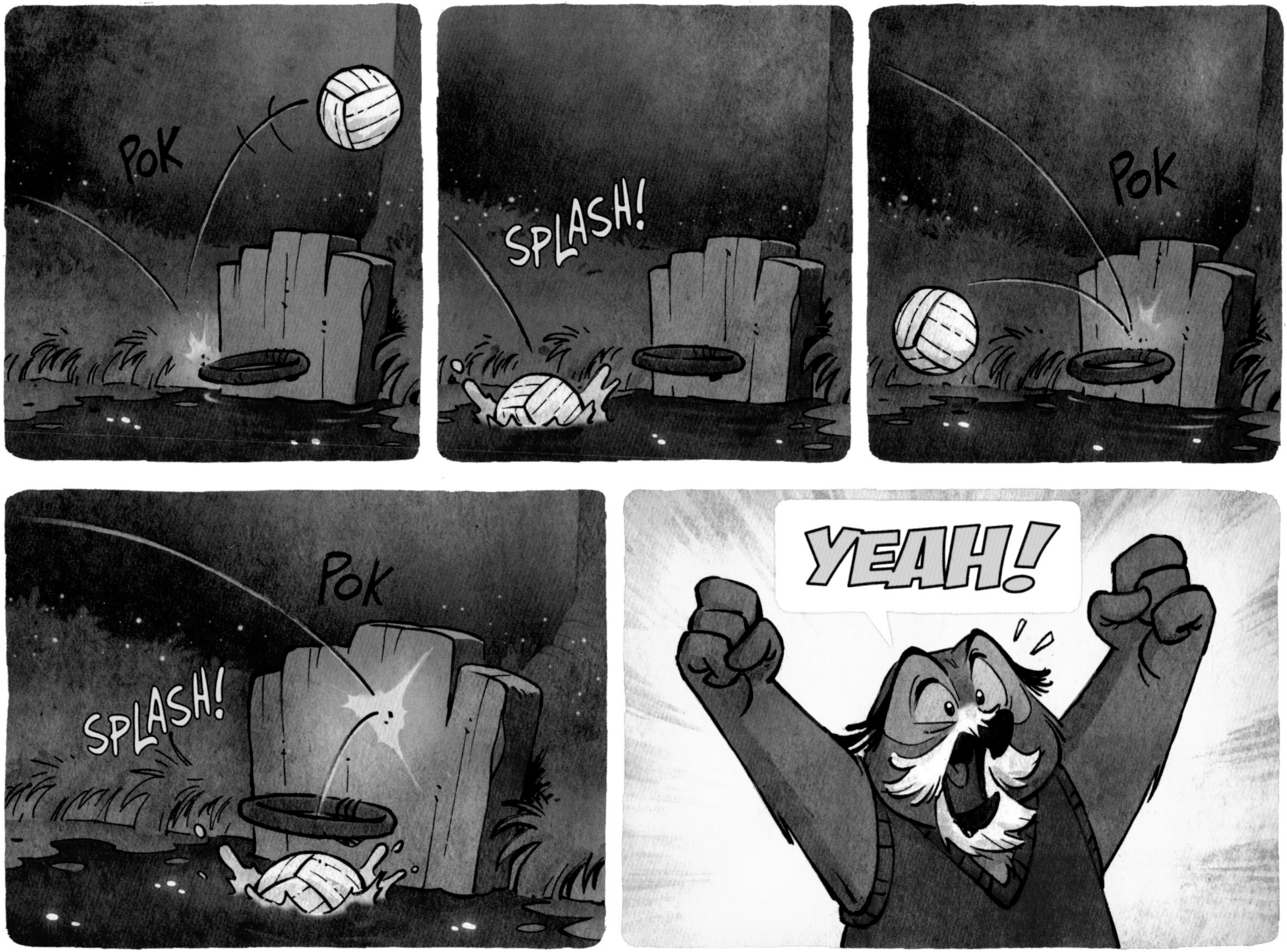
POK
SPLASH!
POK
POK
SPLASH!
YEAH!

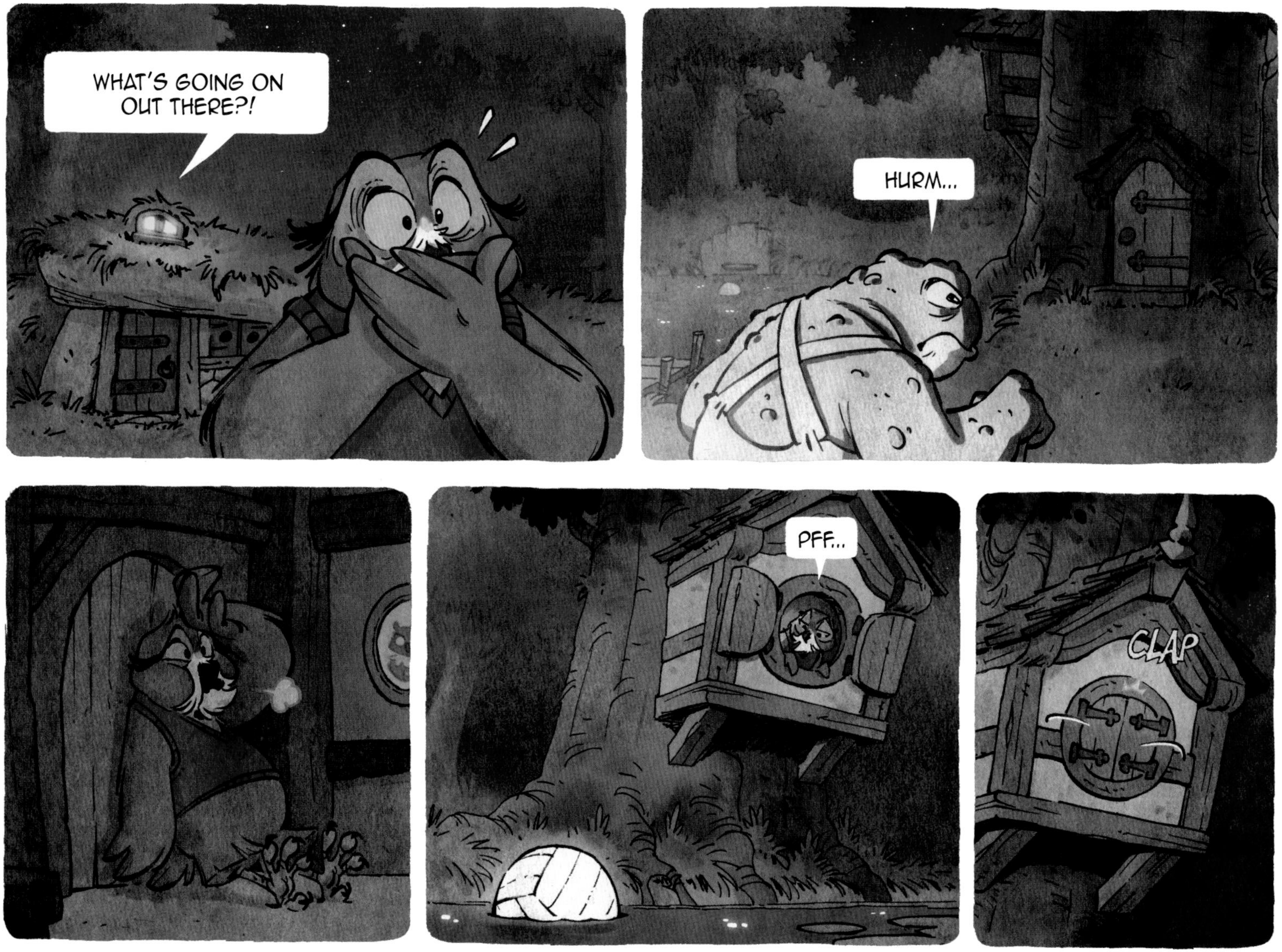
WHAT'S GOING ON OUT THERE?!
HURM...
PFF...
CLAP

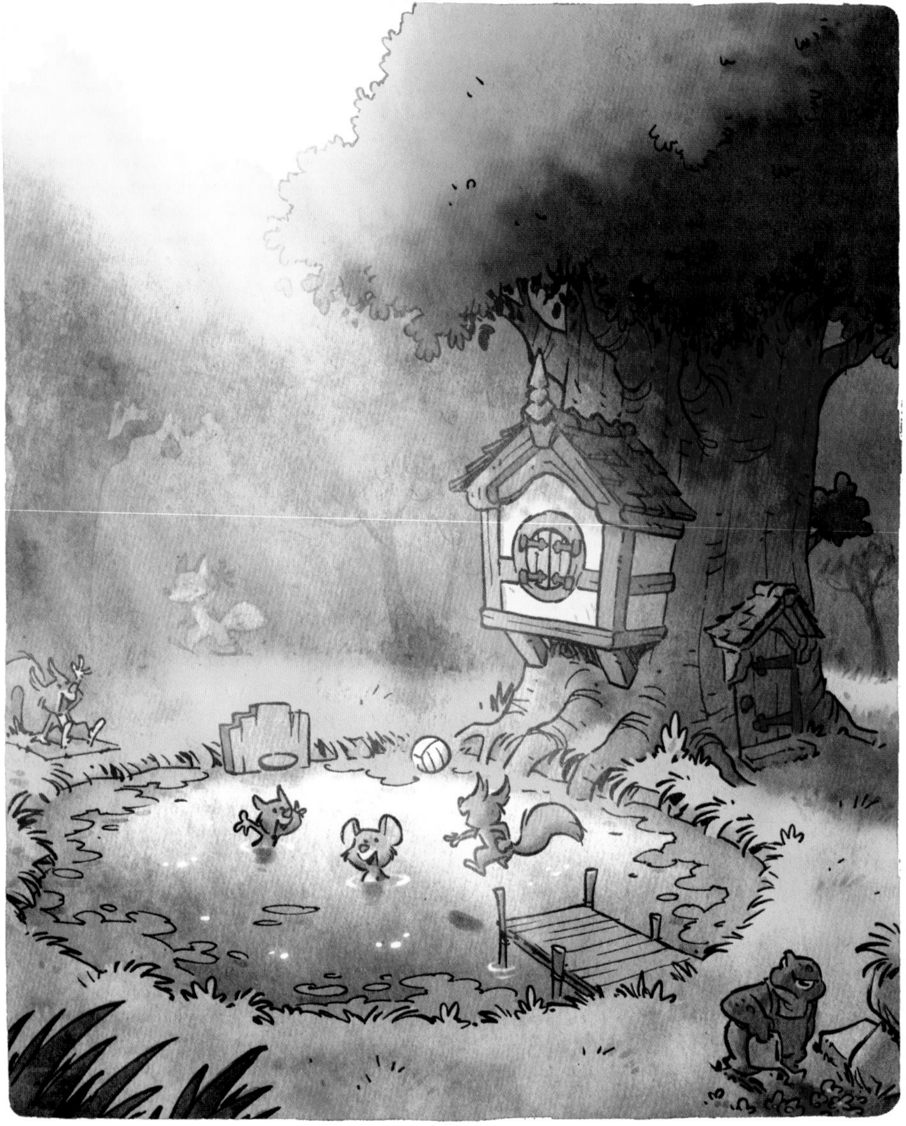

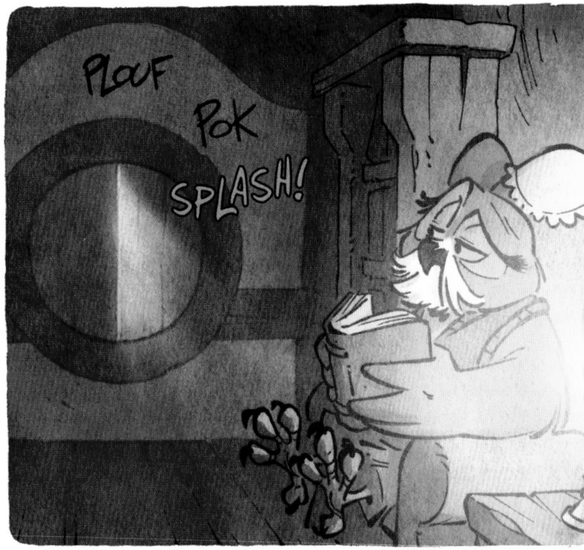
PLOUF
POK
SPLASH!

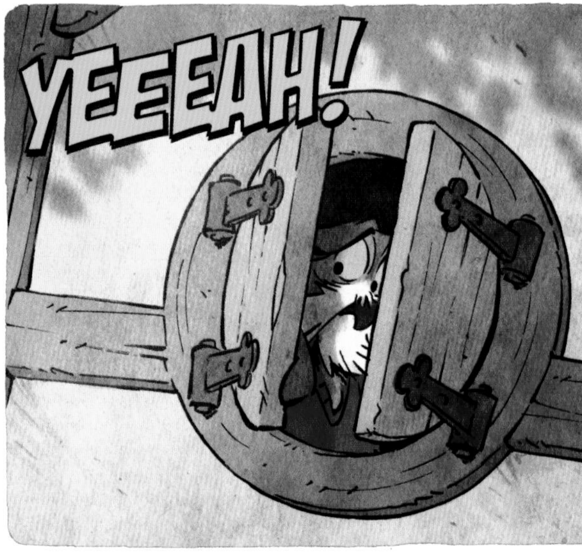
YEEEAH!

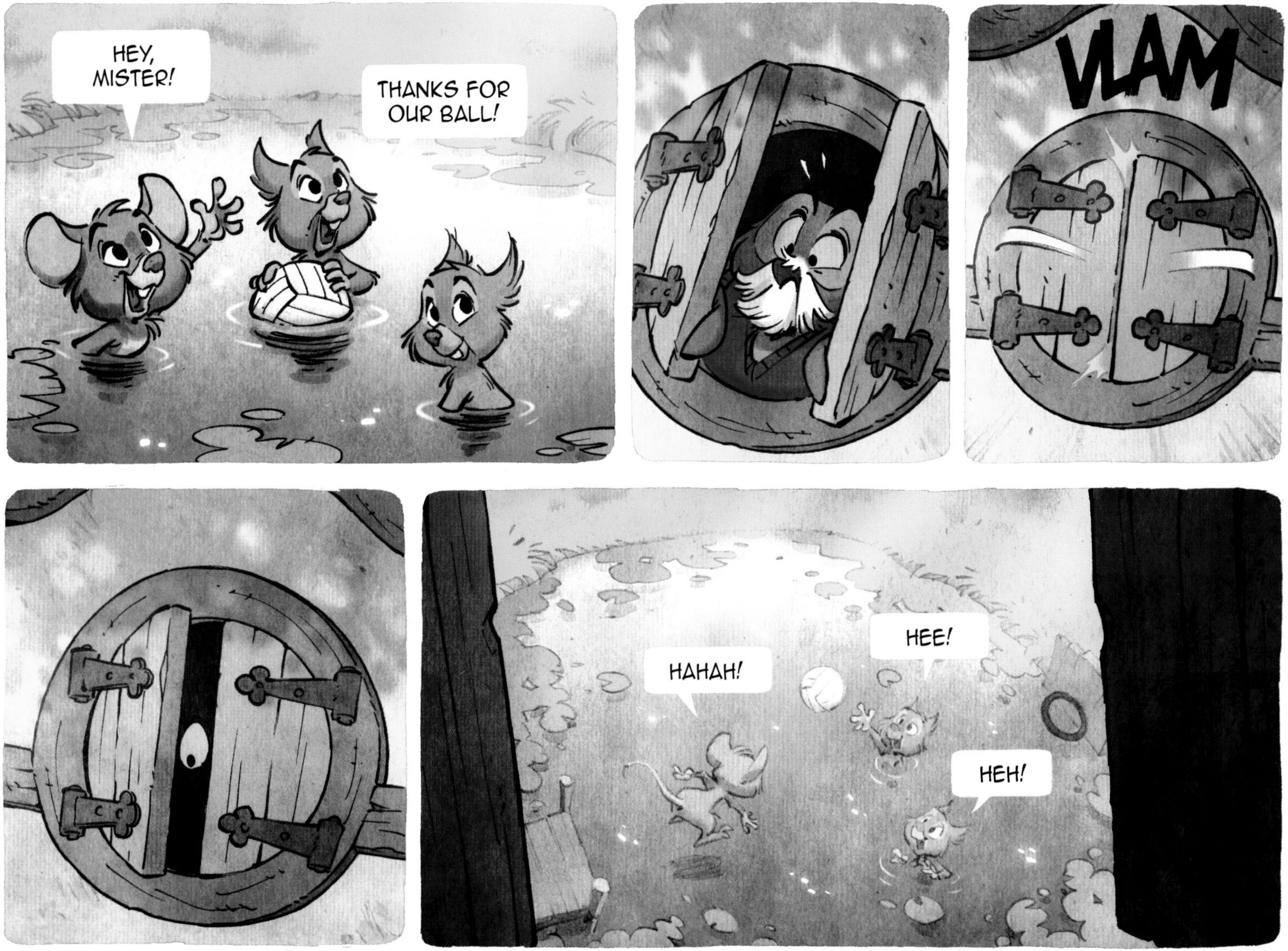
HEY, MISTER!
THANKS FOR OUR BALL!
VLAM
HAHAH!
HEE!
HEH!

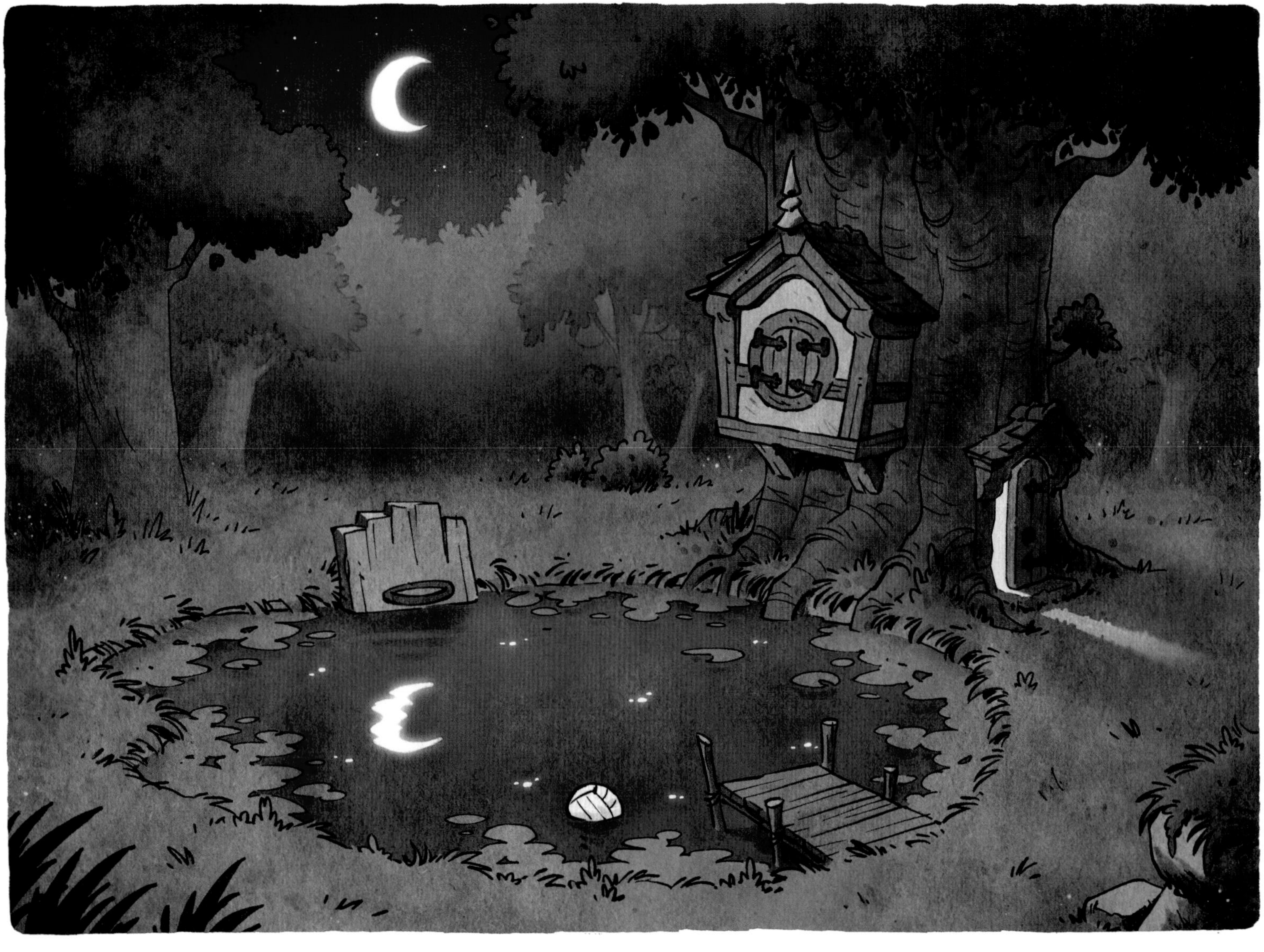

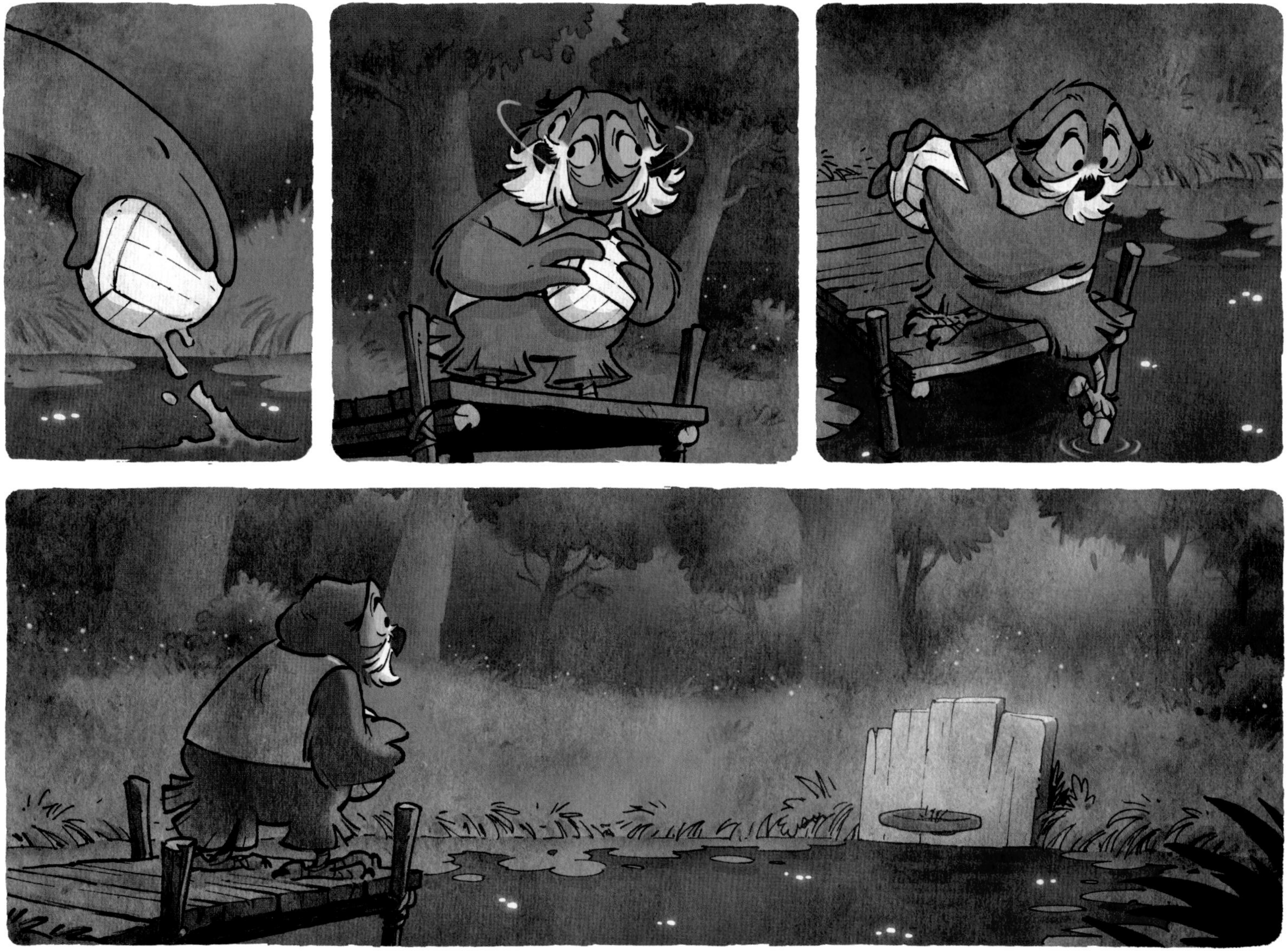

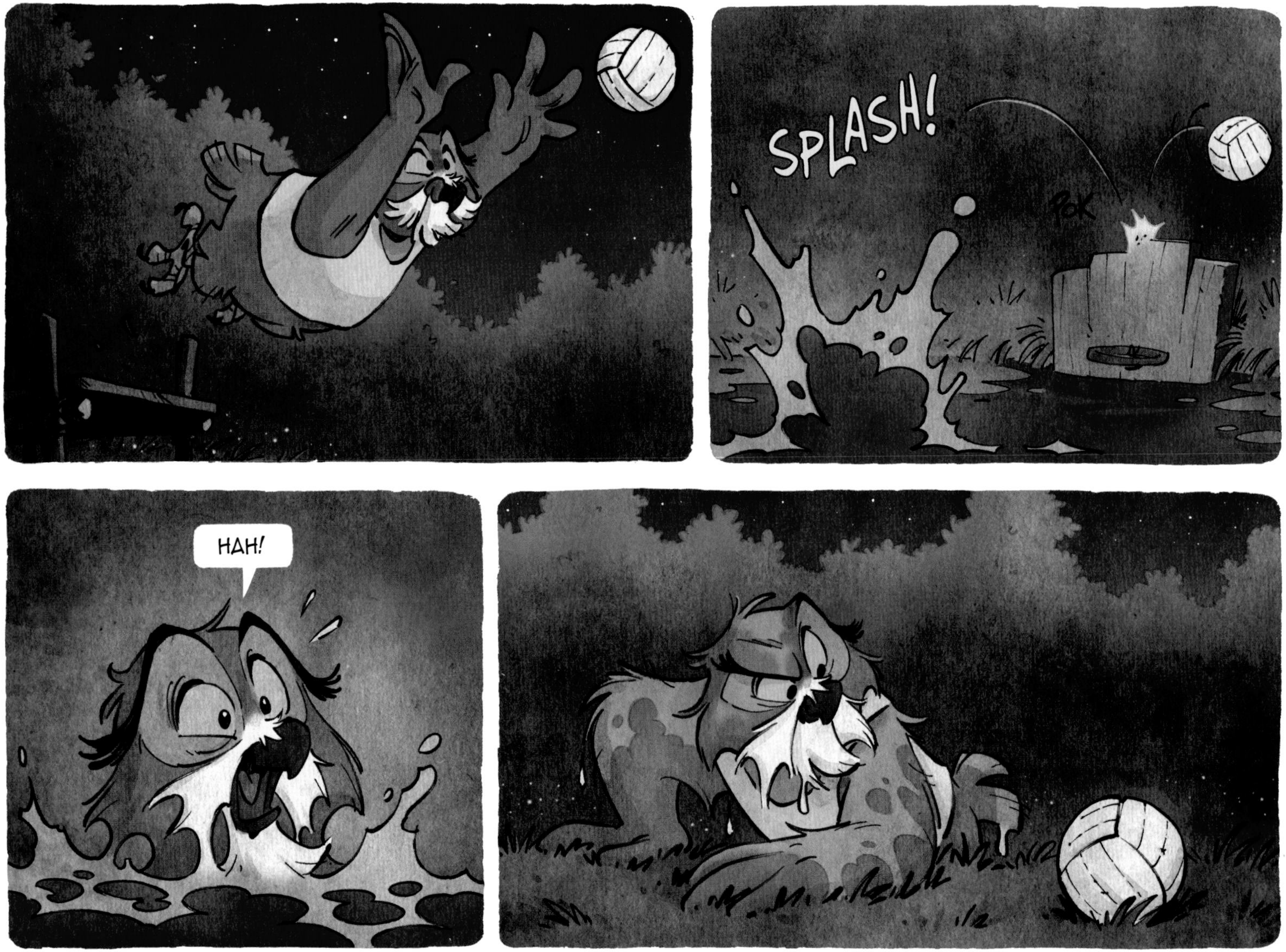
SPLASH!
POK
HAH!

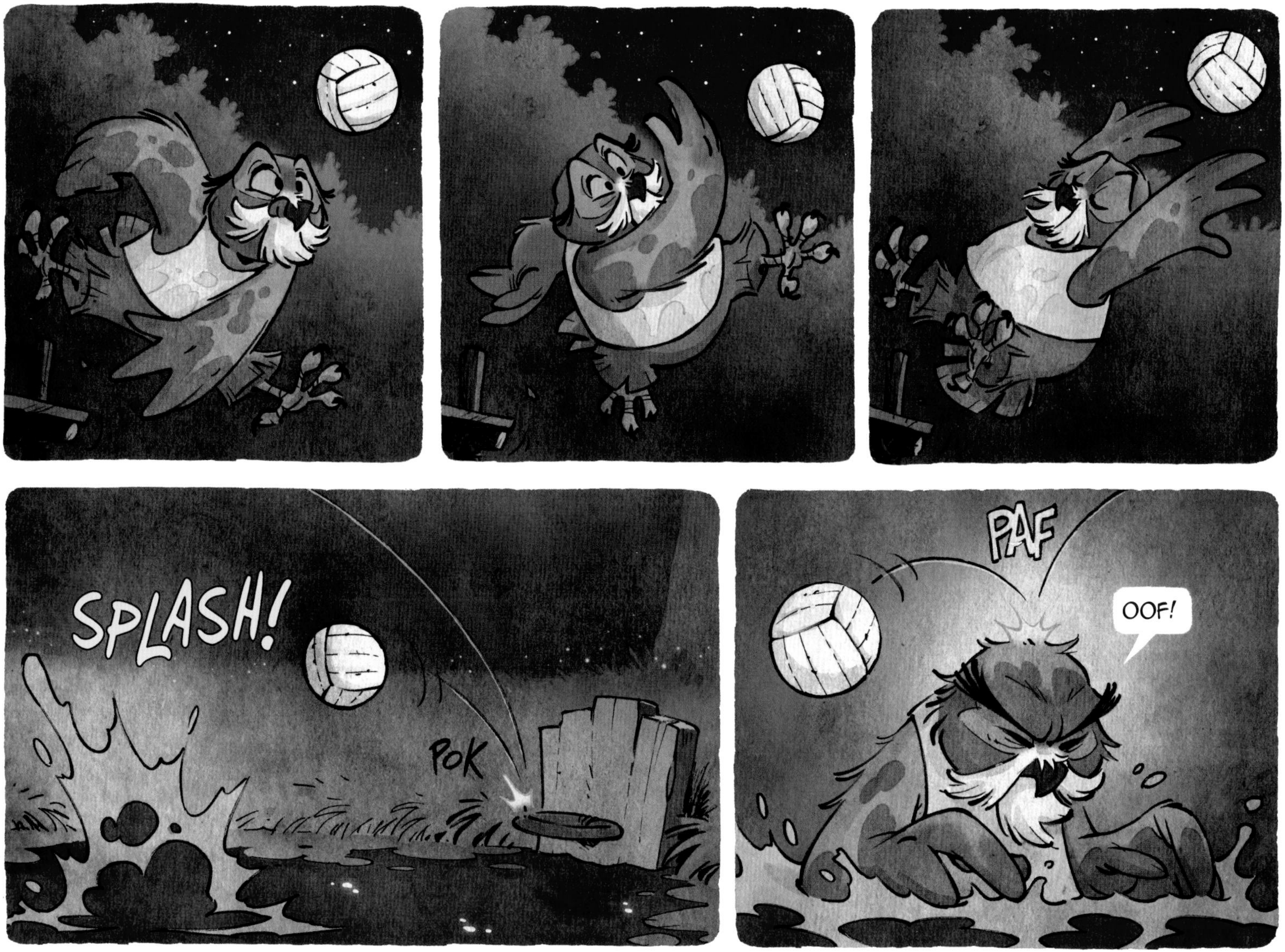
SPLASH!
POK
PAF
OOF!

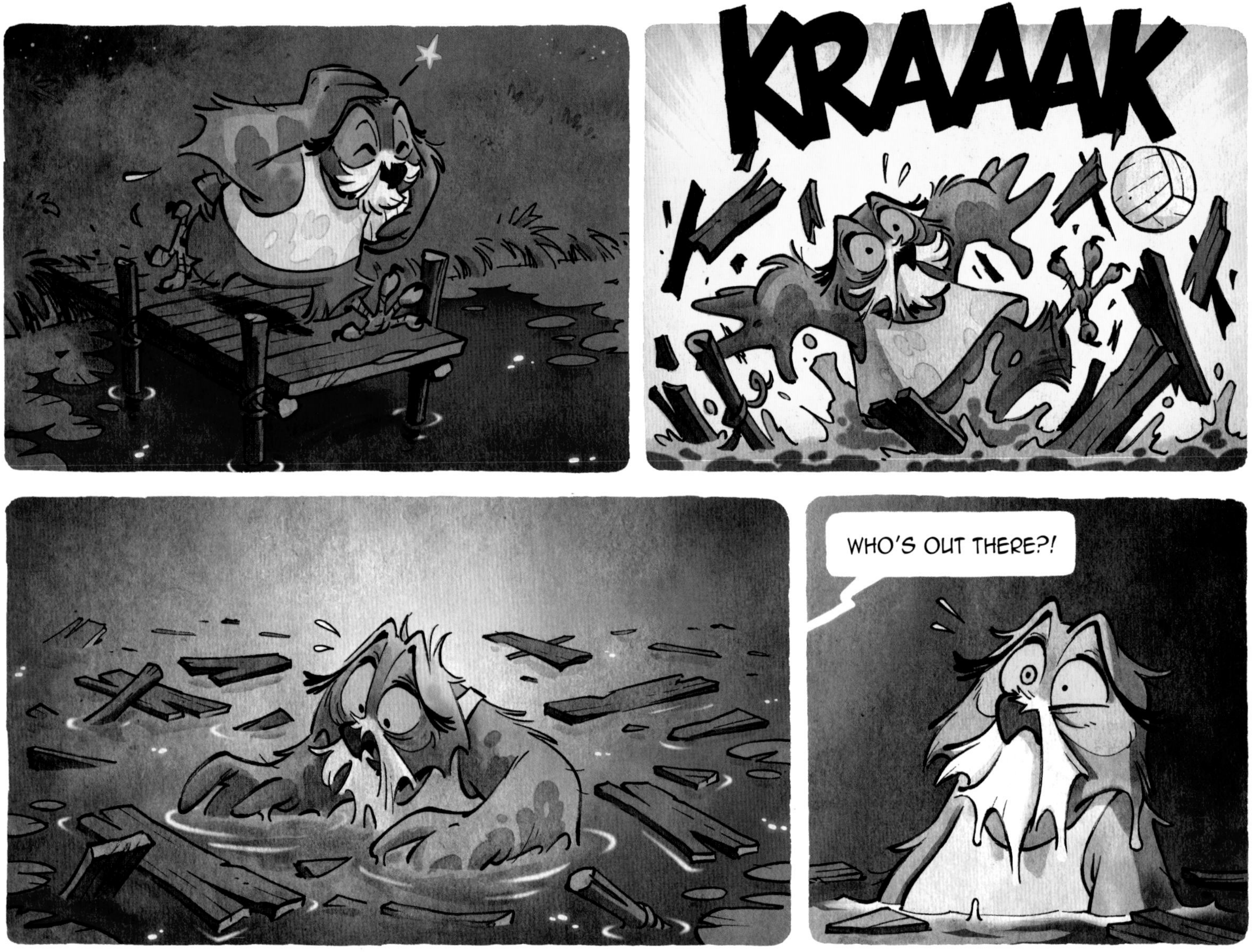
KRAAAK
WHO'S OUT THERE?!

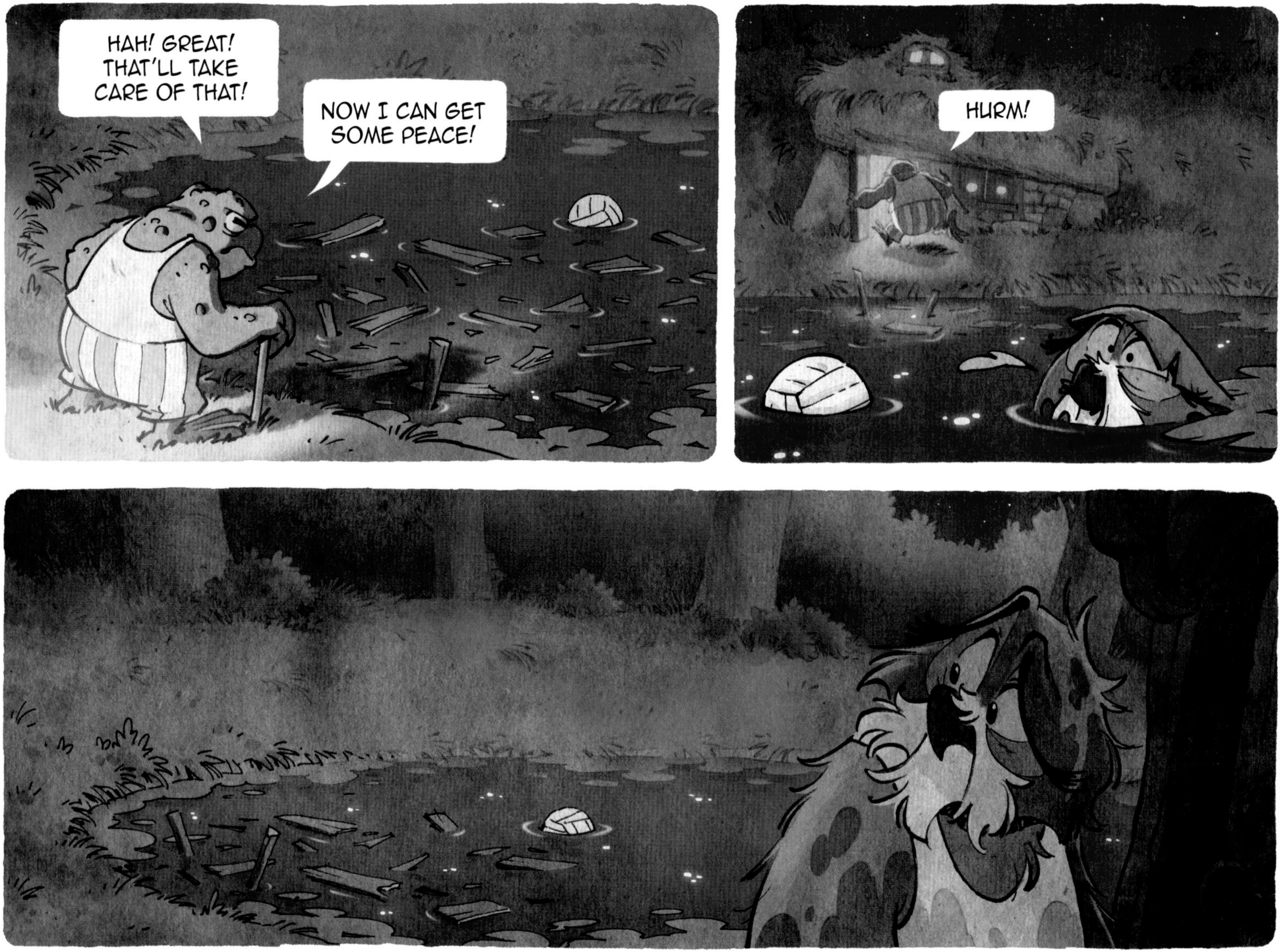
HAH! GREAT! THAT'LL TAKE CARE OF THAT!
NOW I CAN GET SOME PEACE!
HURM!

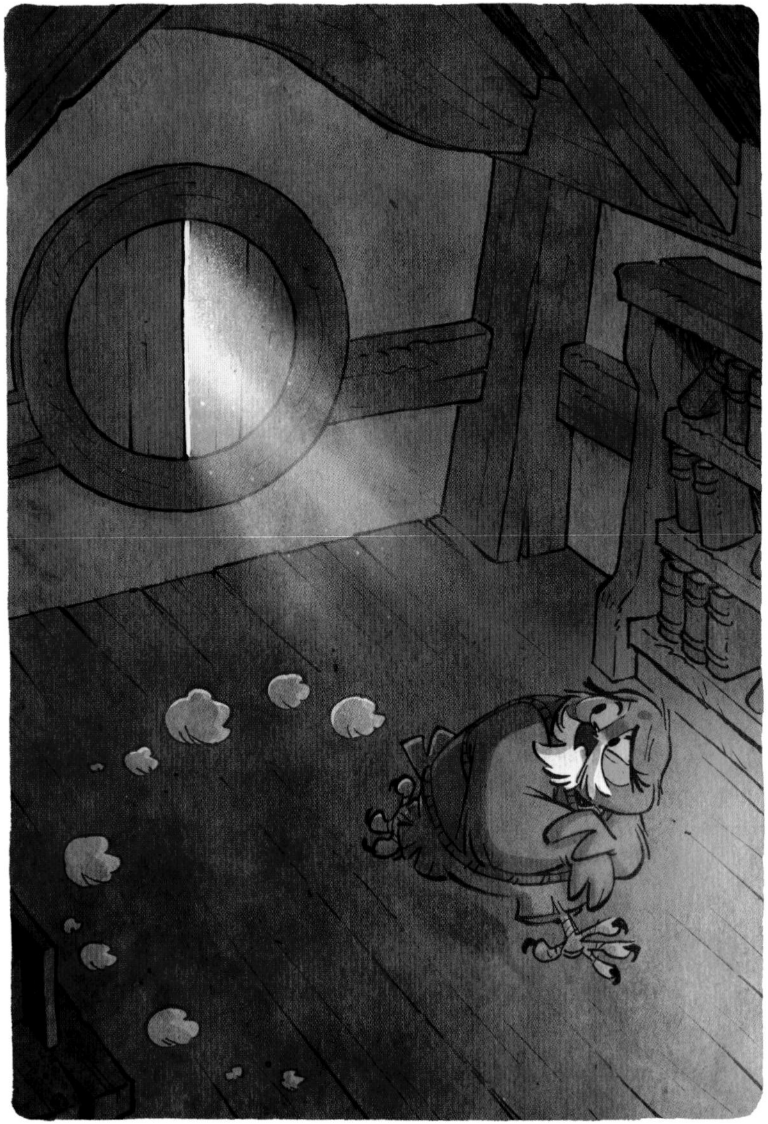

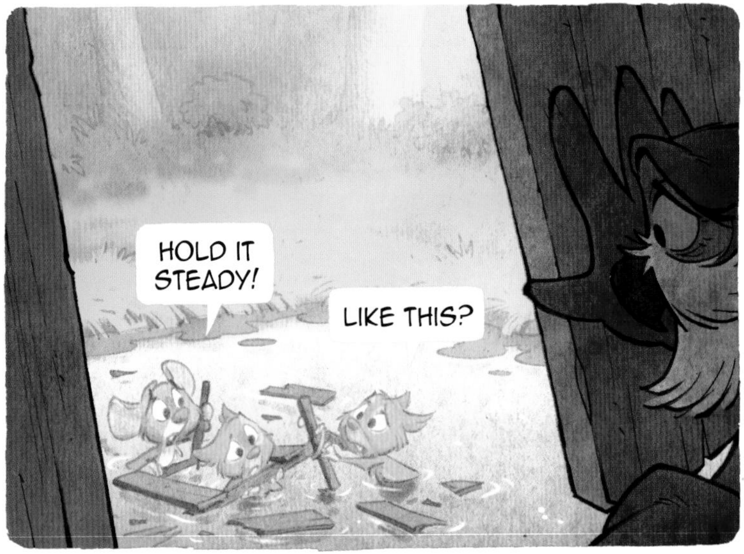
HOLD IT STEADY!
LIKE THIS?

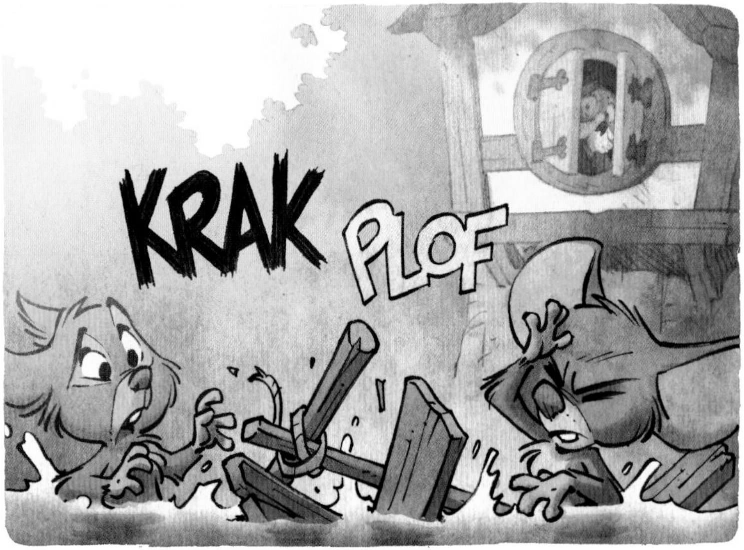
KRAK
PLOF

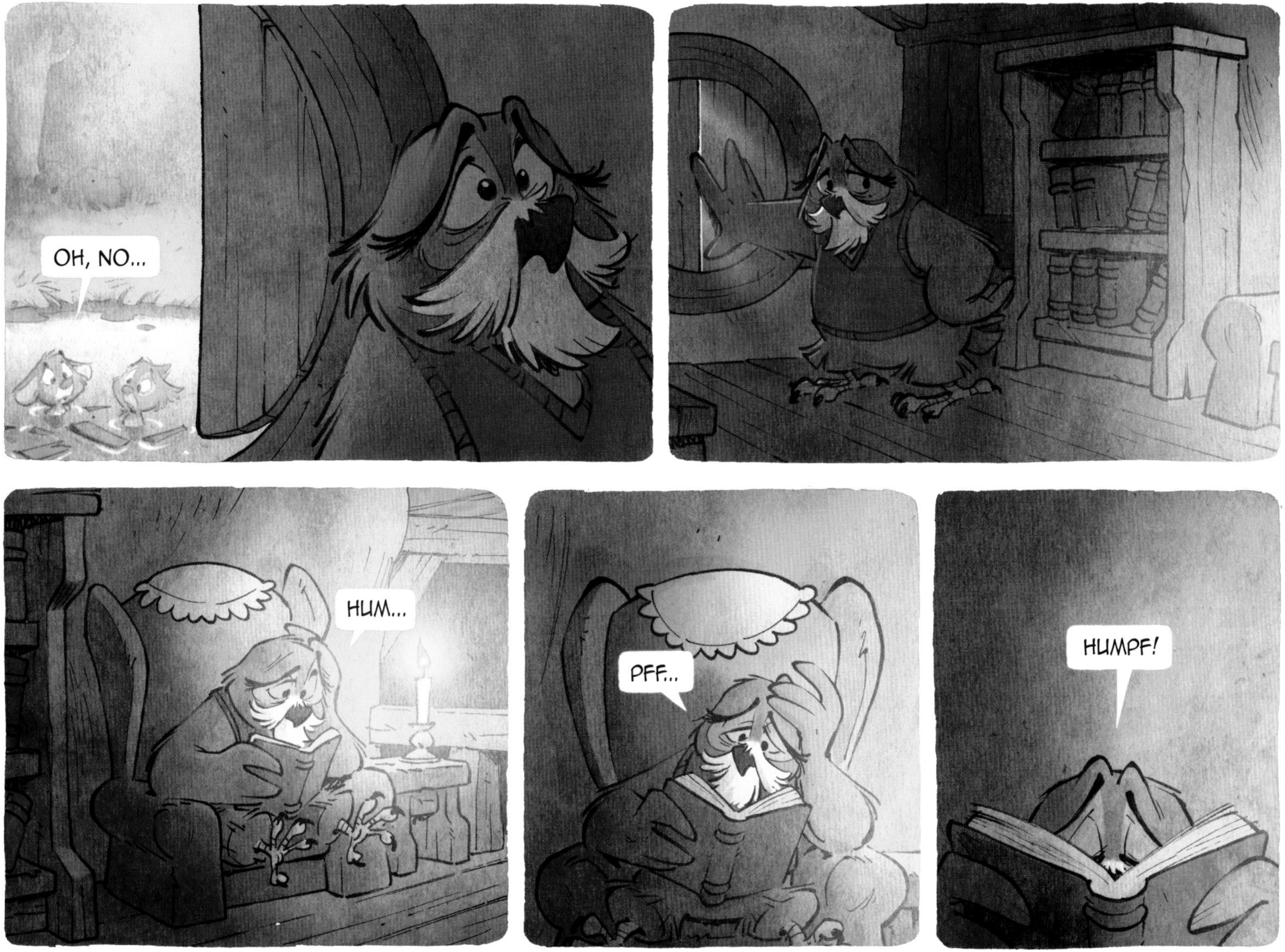
OH, NO...
HUM...
PFF...
HUMPF!

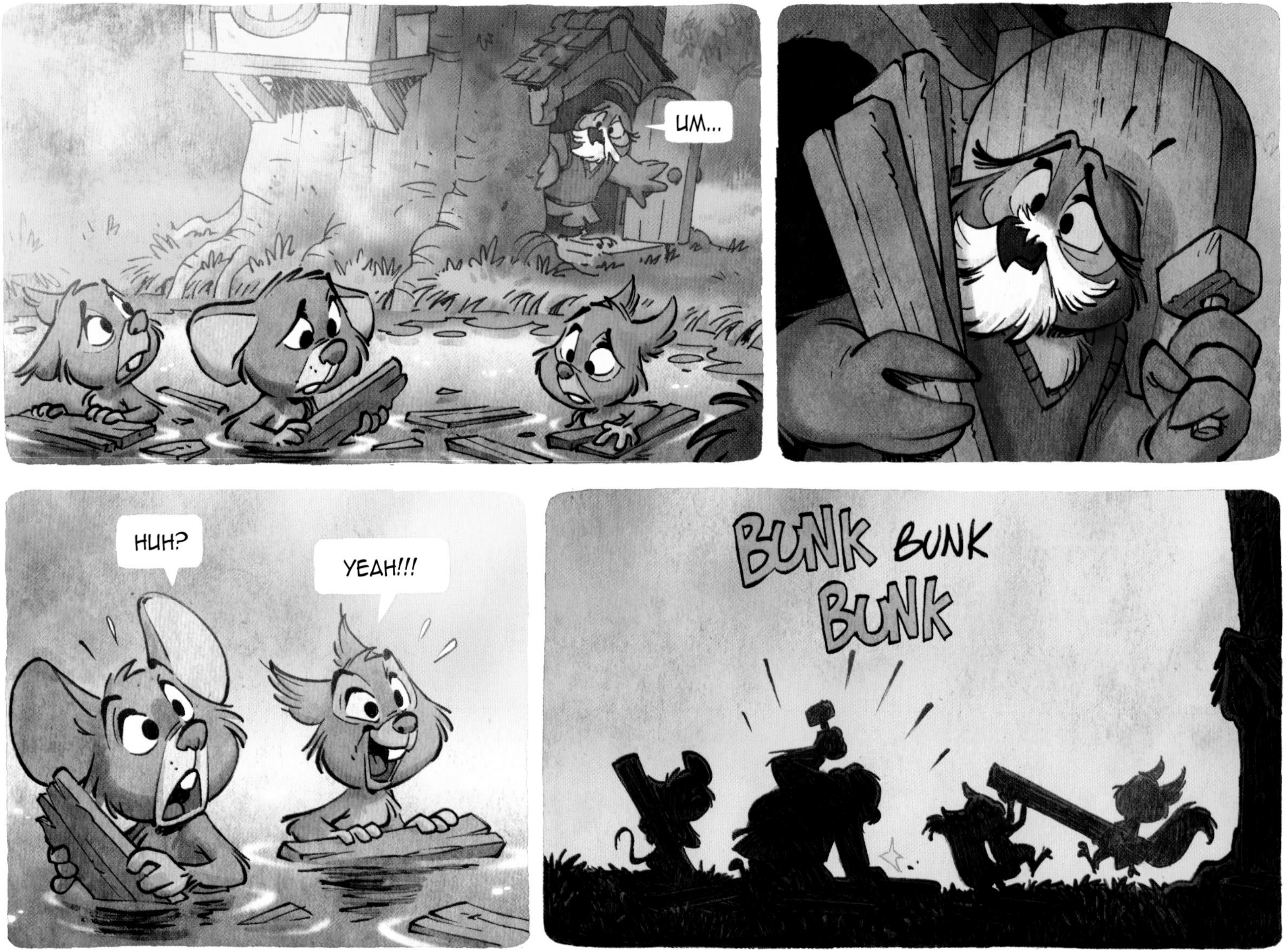
UM...
HUH?
YEAH!!!
BUNK BUNK
BUNK

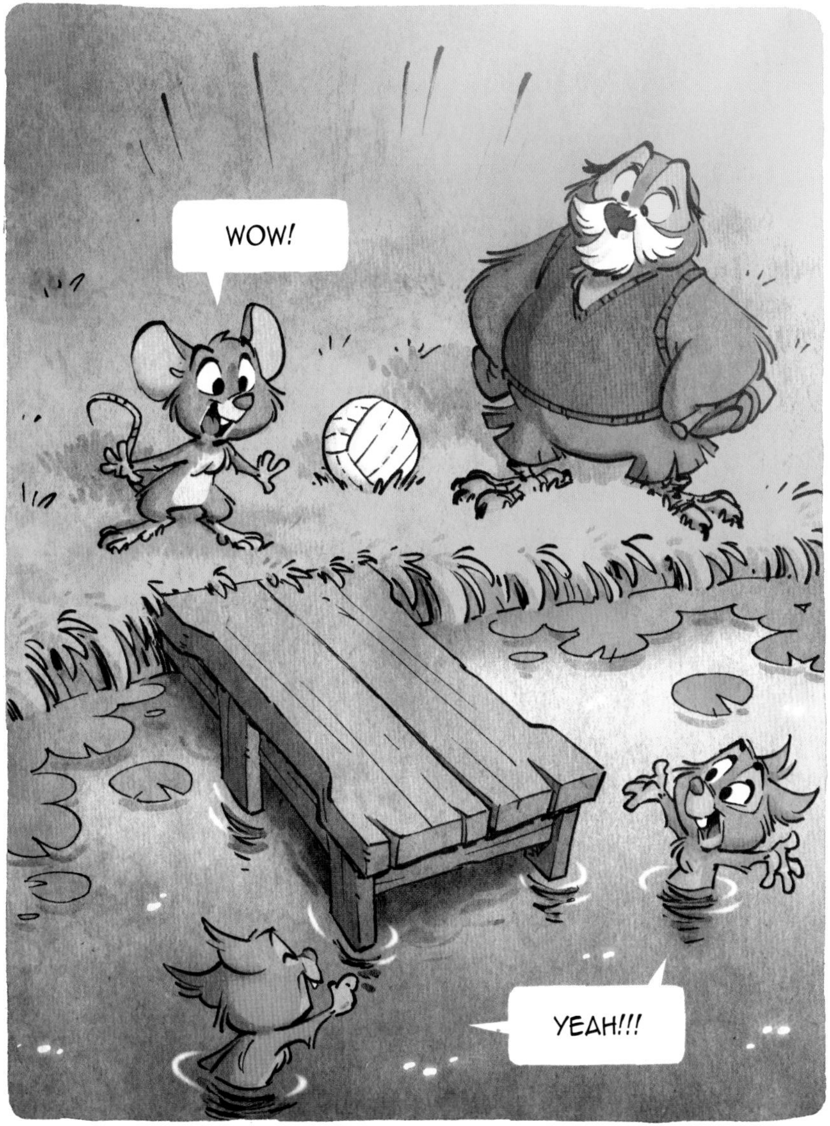
WOW!
YEAH!!!

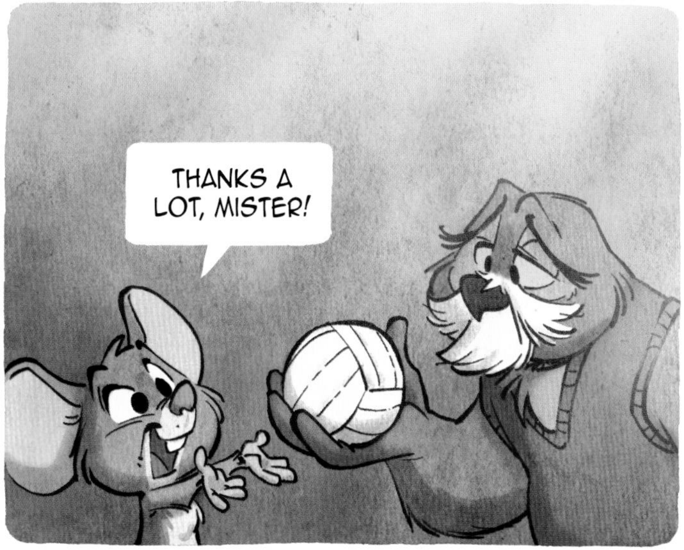
THANKS A LOT, MISTER!

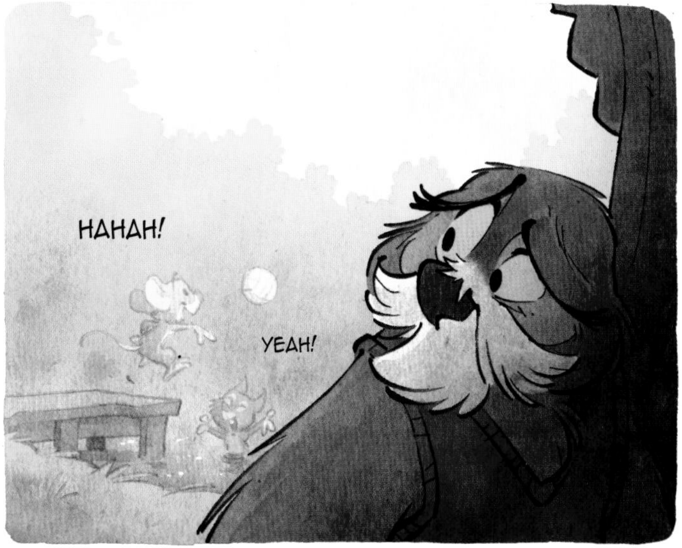
HAHAH!
YEAH!

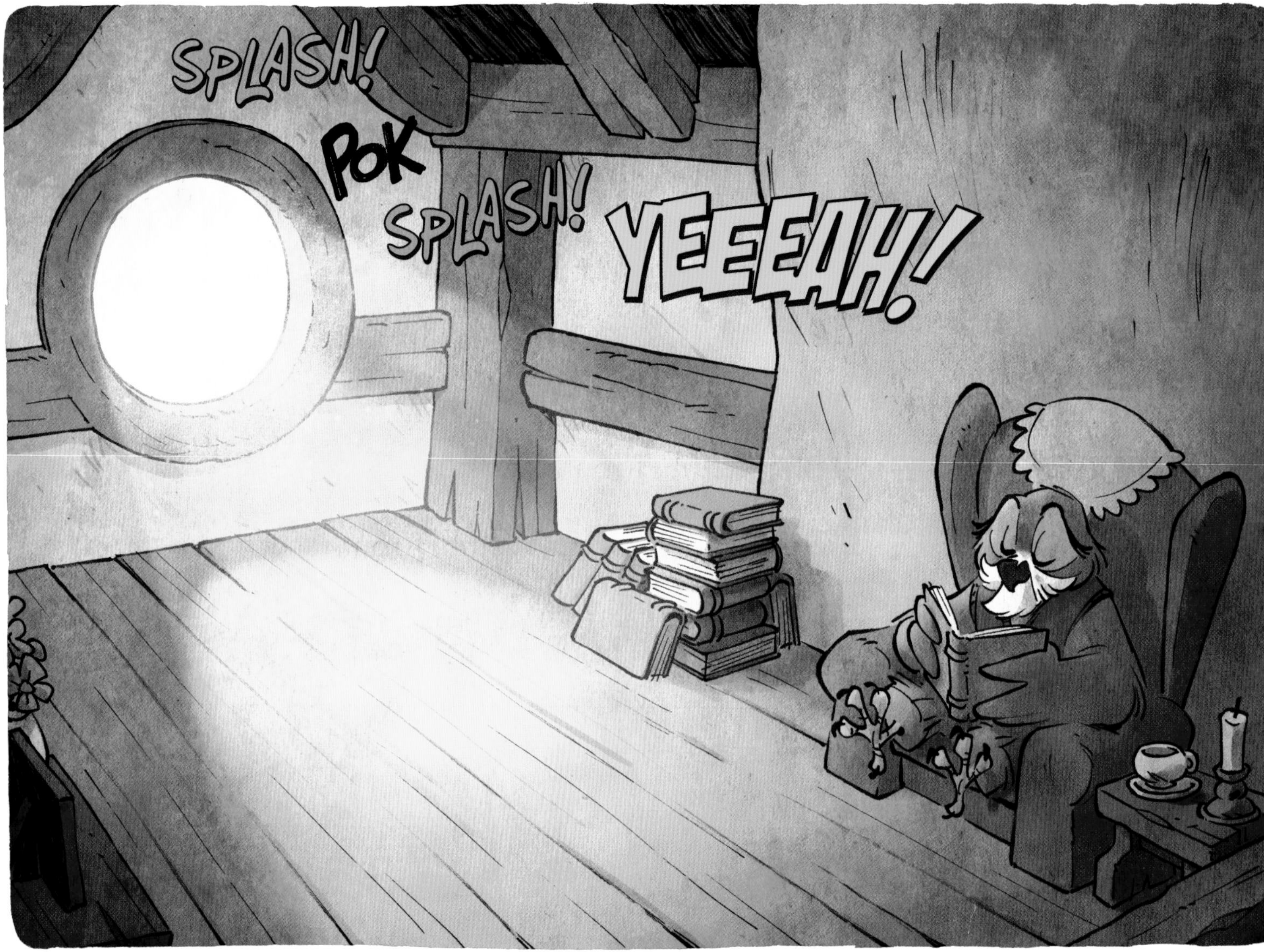
SPLASH!
POK
SPLASH!
YEEEAH!

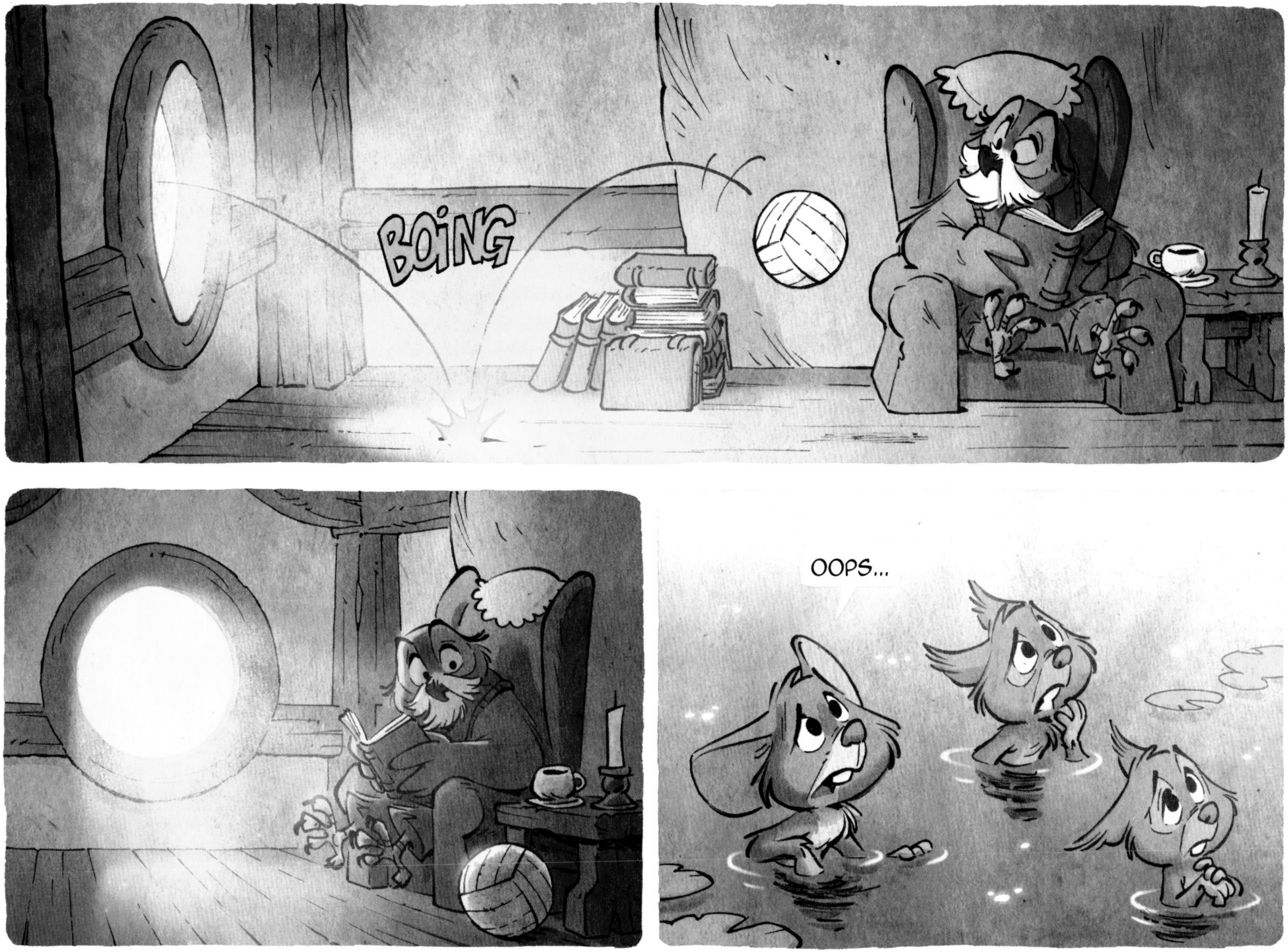
BOING
OOPS...

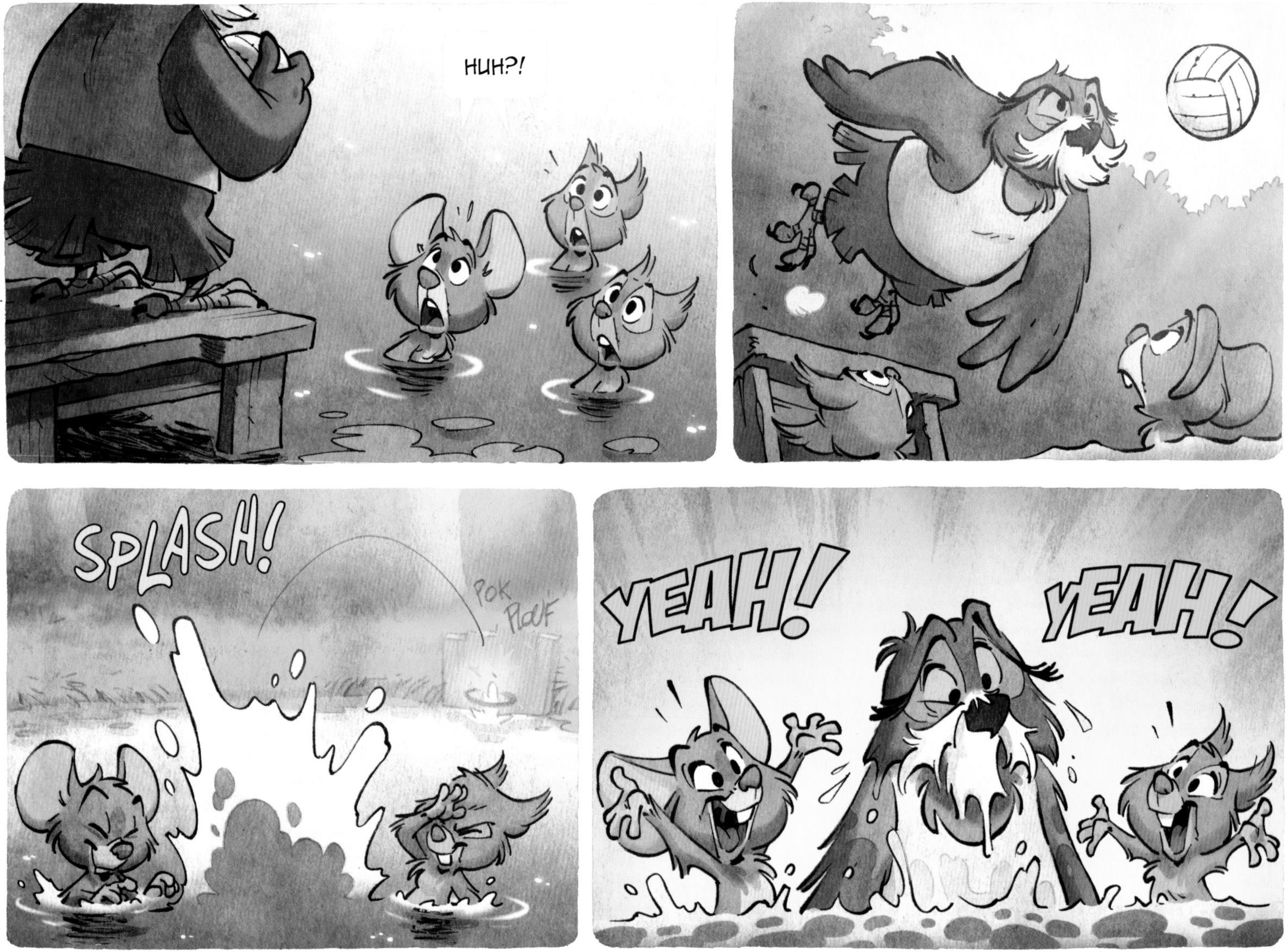
HUH?!
SPLASH!
POK
PLOUF
YEAH!
YEAH!

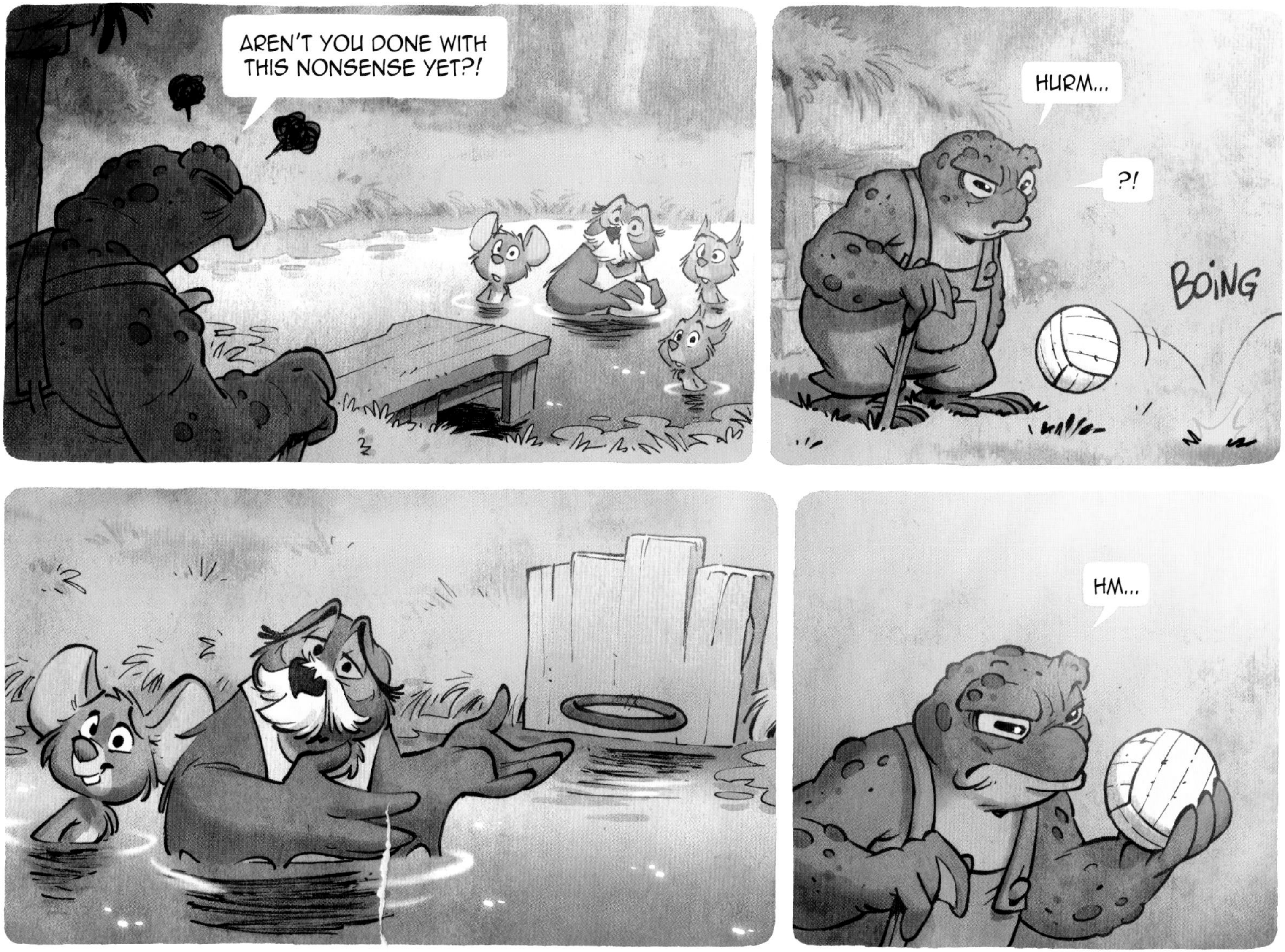
AREN'T YOU DONE WITH THIS NONSENSE YET?!
HURM...
?!
BOING
HM...

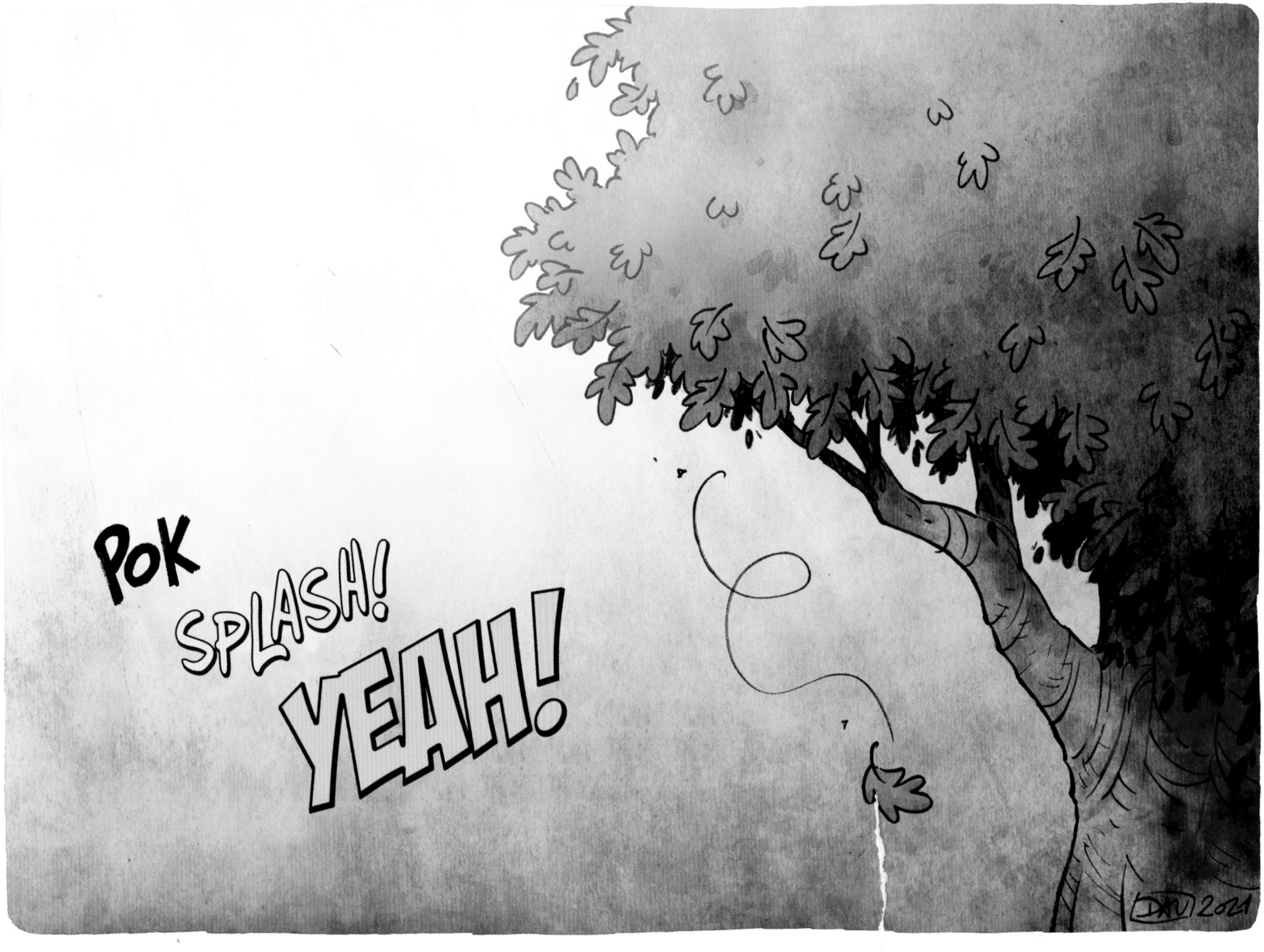
POK
SPLASH!
YEAH!
DAN 2021

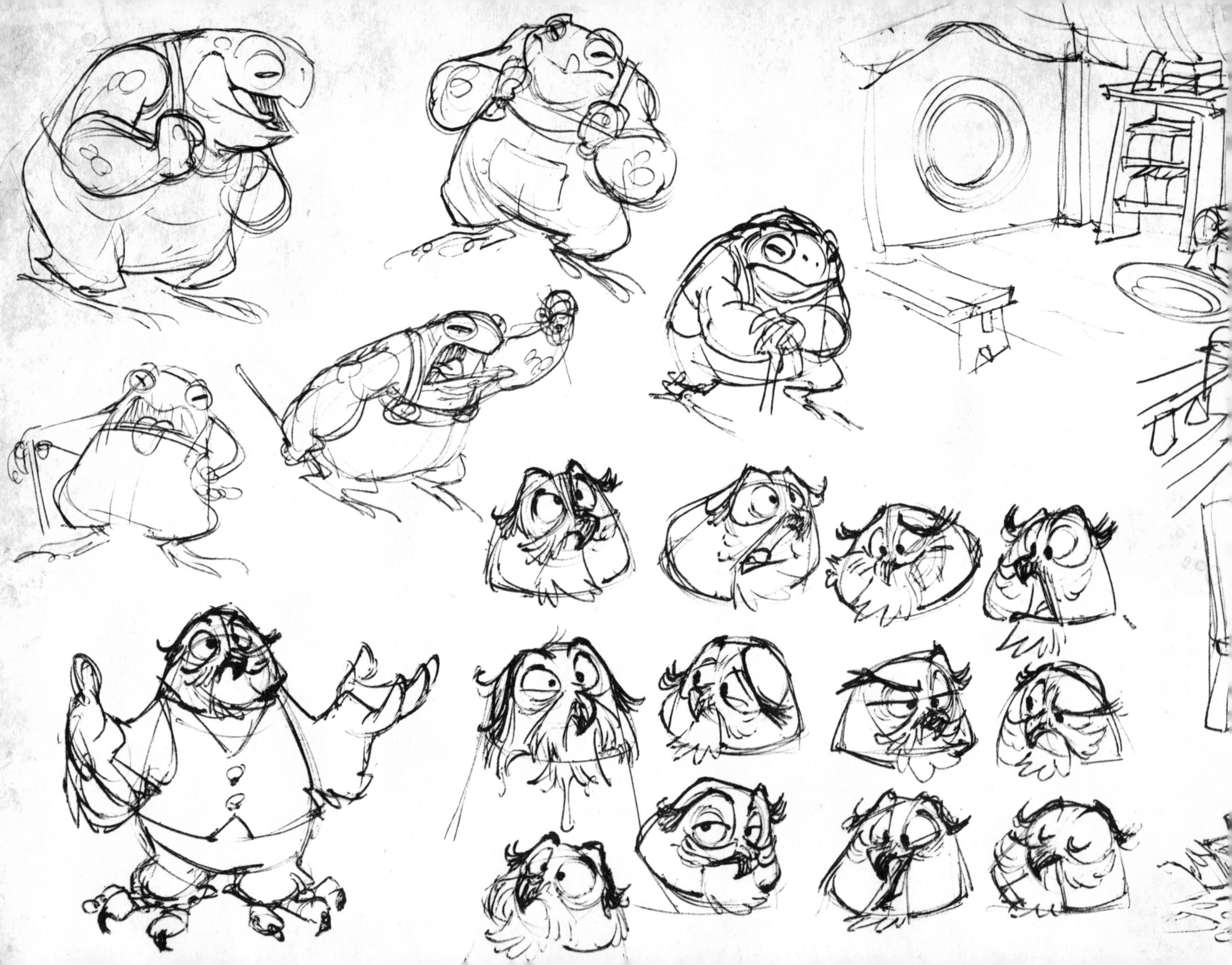